Sammy was asleep when Vanessa placed his car seat in the concrete manger of the life-size nativity scene in front of her sister's house.

She felt a pang of doubt. Was she right to leave the baby with her sister? It was going to be difficult enough to run with the girls. Sammy needed frequent feedings and diaper changes. The girls, at least, could stay quiet when they needed to.

He'd be safer with Alyssa. Wouldn't he? Vanessa looked at the concrete sculptures of Mary and Joseph, poised protectively over the manger. Mary's expression of love and concern seemed to say she'd look over the child.

Vanessa knew she didn't dare linger, no matter how much she wished she could see her sister. She hadn't laid eyes on her since she was kidnapped eight years ago. If Alyssa saw her, she'd have to take the time to explain, and that would endanger them all.

Twin Threat Christmas: Two novellas of twin sisters separated by danger who reunite and find their matches during a dangerous holiday season.

Books by Rachelle McCalla

Love Inspired Suspense

Survival Instinct
Troubled Waters
Out on a Limb
Danger on Her Doorstep
Dead Reckoning
**Princess in Peril*
**Protecting the Princess*
The Detective's Secret Daughter
*Prince Incognito
**The Missing Monarch*
†*Defending the Duchess*
†*Royal Heist*
†*Royal Wedding Threat*
Twin Threat Christmas

Love Inspired Historical

†*A Royal Marriage*
†*The Secret Princess*

*Reclaiming the Crown
†Protecting the Crown

RACHELLE McCALLA

writes books with kissing, praying and dead bodies. She is a pastor's wife, mother of four and holds a Master of Divinity degree. When she is not writing, she can be found sneaking vegetables into her kids' food. Sometimes she even sneaks vegetables into her books. That may explain why her readers have such a healthy glow.

TWIN THREAT CHRISTMAS

RACHELLE MCCALLA

HARLEQUIN® LOVE INSPIRED® SUSPENSE

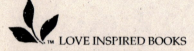 LOVE INSPIRED BOOKS

Recycling programs for this product may not exist in your area.

ISBN-13: 978-0-373-44632-2

Twin Threat Christmas

Copyright © 2014 by Harlequin Books S.A.

The publisher acknowledges the copyright holder of the individual works as follows:

One Silent Night
Copyright © 2014 by Rachelle McCalla

Danger in the Manger
Copyright © 2014 by Rachelle McCalla

www.Harlequin.com

Printed in U.S.A.

CONTENTS

ONE SILENT NIGHT

To all who have ever been lost.
May you find your way home again.

Are not two sparrows sold for a penny?
Yet not one of them will fall to the ground
outside your Father's care. And even the very hairs
of your head are all numbered. So don't be afraid;
you are worth more than many sparrows.
—*Matthew* 10:29–31

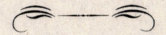

ONE

She couldn't breathe. Vanessa had feared this moment for years, envisioned it repeatedly over the past few months, watched it play out time after time in her nightmares. And yet, for all its familiarity, nothing could match the terror she felt now that it was actually happening.

It was worse than she'd imagined it.

The black Land Rover pulled into the middle of the driveway.

The middle! Why block the entire double-lane driveway? Why today?

Because they didn't want anyone to get out alive, that was why.

"Mommy, Mommy!" Emma tugged at Vanessa's shirt. "My apple juice!"

Vanessa sucked in enough air to speak. "Yes, Emma. I have your apple juice right here. You can drink it in the car. We're going to do the quiet drill again. Remember the quiet drill?"

To Vanessa's relief, her four-year-old's eyes lit up. "The quiet drill. Yes! But Sammy is napping."

"I know, sweetheart." Vanessa handed her daughter the sippy cup of juice. "It will be okay. Can you get your jacket on? And tell Abby. Remember to whisper. Everything will be okay." Vanessa spoke the last words as much for her own reassurance as for Emma's. She gave her daughter an encouraging smile, then glanced back out the basement-level window in time to see an all-too-familiar pair of black shoes looking not too out of place in the quiet suburban cul-de-sac.

And boots. Two pairs. No, three.

Virgil had extra guns with him today.

Of course he did. He'd told Jeff on his last visit there wouldn't be another warning. His money or his life…and the lives of Vanessa and the children.

As always, Jeff had made the deal without consulting her. Vanessa had no intention of letting him bargain with their lives. She'd been preparing ever since, hiding emergency supplies in the garage, ready to go. Drilling the children on a swift and silent evacuation. She was ready—as prepared as anyone ever could be.

But why did Virgil have to park in the middle of the driveway?

The doorbell echoed through the house, and Vanessa flew into action. She might not have much time. Sure, Virgil liked to talk. She hoped he'd try to threaten Jeff a little longer in hopes of squeezing the money out of him, but there was every chance the mobster—gangster, whatever he was, Vanessa had never really wanted to know—might drag the kids out first in an effort to make his argument more compelling.

Sammy was still asleep, just as Emma said. Vanessa scooped up the ten-month-old and set him as gently as possible into his waiting car seat.

This was the part of her escape plan that troubled her most, one of the biggest reasons she'd never been brave enough—or desperate enough—to attempt to escape with the kids before. Abby and Emma could be depended upon to flee in silence. But if Sam cried, he would give away their position, and she couldn't stop him.

His rosebud lips opened in protest as Vanessa tucked one arm through the five-point harness. Prepared, Vanessa slipped a pacifier into his open mouth and prayed.

Please, Lord. If ever I needed Your help, it's today.

Sammy made a grumpy face, but his eyes stayed closed and he started sucking.

Gently, Vanessa pulled his other arm through its strap, buckled him in and hoisted up the car seat, all but running to the stairs that led to the garage.

As she rose toward the second floor, she could hear Virgil arguing with Jeff in the living room upstairs, their voices muffled but angry. They were in the house.

She had to hurry, and reached for the forbidden keys. Jeff almost never allowed her to drive, not unless he was with her, his gun at his side to make sure she didn't try to get away from him. That the keys were on a peg by the garage at all was a recent concession, made only after Virgil's latest threat.

That Jeff had agreed meant he, too, understood Virgil wasn't messing around. Jeff had kept her tied up for the first year after he'd kidnapped her, only allowing her a tiny bit of freedom in the locked basement after Abby was born. Even now, he'd strictly told her she wasn't to try to leave the basement without him.

But still the keys were there. The door that led to the garage was unlocked. On some level, whether consciously or not, Jeff had allowed her a means of running for her life—even if it meant escaping from him, something he'd long told her she could never do.

Vanessa grabbed the fat ring of keys as she slipped through the door to the garage.

Abby and Emma looked at her from inside the Sequoia with anxious eyes as Vanessa carried Sammy into the garage. "Did you get the bags?" she asked her seven-year-old as she settled the infant car seat into place.

"Yes," Abby whispered, true to the plan.

A quick glance in the third-row seat confirmed everything was in place.

Everything but the enormous vehicle blocking the driveway.

Vanessa climbed into the driver's seat. "Everybody buckled?" she asked, latching her own seat belt.

"Yes, Mommy."

Now what? The next step of the drill was to back out of the driveway as quickly as possible, to get away before Virgil or his men could get off a shot. But with the house on one side of the driveway and the steep, terraced side of the landscaped hill on the immediate other side, there was no way out of the garage except the driveway, and Virgil had blocked it. The Land Rover was worse than a solid wall behind them.

A solid wall.

Vanessa looked at the wall in front of her. Plywood sheathing, two-by-fours spaced widely apart. And on the other side, vinyl siding.

How hard could it be?

She didn't have time to find out. She didn't have options. There was certain death in every other direction. Jeff had forced her to witness enough of Virgil's "disciplinary measures" to know his warnings weren't empty threats.

Maybe she should have tried to get away before, even years before, but Jeff had always made certain that wasn't possible. Even once Abby was born and Vanessa wasn't bound with ropes or chains, it became too difficult to escape with a baby in tow. Jeff kept them locked in the basement whenever he wasn't home to guard over her. For the past seven years, her priority had been giving her children a normal childhood—or as close to normal as she could provide under Jeff's armed supervision.

Jeff's threats echoed through her thoughts even now. Jeff knew too much about her family. He'd threatened to torture and kill her grandfather and sister, to take her children from her, malign her as a bad mother, claiming she'd lied to him about her real age and identity

No, Vanessa hadn't dared try to escape, not as long as

Jeff was alive to come after her or give information for Virgil to track down everyone she held dear.

But this time, Virgil's threat was bigger than Jeff's. Virgil had promised the last time that if he had to come back, he wouldn't let any of them live, not even Jeff—which meant Jeff couldn't come after her or tell Virgil anything that might help him find her.

In some ways the criminal was freeing her.

If only his vehicle wasn't barring the way. It was far, far too late to call the police, even if Vanessa had any hope they'd let her keep her children. No, Jeff had made clear what she'd lose if she tried to get the law on her side. Her word against his, and that of his associates.

There was only one way out of the garage

Dear Lord, please let this work.

"Okay, girls, tuck your heads like I told you." Vanessa had originally planned for the girls to lay their heads on their laps, covered by their arms, to protect them from possible gunfire as she backed down the driveway past the living-room picture window. But a tucked-head position might be just as protective going the other direction.

She had a good ten feet of empty storage space in front of her, maybe more. Normally she would never start a vehicle inside a closed garage, but they wouldn't be in there for more than a few seconds.

She turned the key, threw the SUV into gear and stomped on the gas, throwing one arm up over her face and pinching her eyes shut, holding tight to the steering wheel with her other hand. The vehicle leaped forward, slamming into the wall, pushing through it with the sound of splintering wood and cracking boards.

"Mommy! You drove through the wall!"

"I know, Emma. It's okay." Vanessa steered around the girls' playhouse. The Sequoia lurched across the sandbox, flattening the tall privacy fence that had long held them prisoner, clipping the neighbor's back bushes en route to the street.

The big tires lumbered down the curb. Vanessa cruised down the familiar boulevard, four blocks, five, and came to a stop at the traffic light. She checked for oncoming traffic. Finding the way clear, she turned right onto the busy street, checked her rearview mirror for any sign of the Land Rover and breathed the tiniest sigh of relief.

No sign of them. Yet.

But Virgil and his men could come after them any moment.

The front of the vehicle was probably scratched and dented, but the windshield hadn't even cracked. The girls were wide-eyed but silent. Sammy was whimpering. Still, most important, they were alive.

Alert!
Abducted children in danger!

Eric stopped flipping through the channels on the cabin's relic of a television as the screen flashed pictures of two little girls and a baby. A boy. Samuel.

The reporter rattled off the details in a matter-of-fact voice. "The Nelson children are believed to be with their mother. Their father's body was found this evening. Authorities at this time are assuming he was shot by his wife, who took the children following a domestic dispute."

"So what's the forecast?" Debbi, Eric's younger sister, bounded into the room behind him, then stopped short. "Oh, no."

"They are believed to be traveling in a brown Toyota Sequoia, which may have front-end damage. Authorities believe the woman drove through the back wall of the garage as she left."

The scene on the screen switched from the children's faces to a picture of an SUV superimposed over footage of splintered two-by-fours and the busted-out back wall of a garage.

The reporter turned to a man standing in front of a black Land Rover. "This is Chicago businessman Virgil Greenwood, who discovered the body of Jeffrey Nelson at Mr. Nelson's Barrington home this evening. Mr. Greenwood, can you tell us what happened?"

Virgil Greenwood, a middle-aged man in a business suit, nodded soberly. "Mr. Nelson and I were supposed to have a business dinner together today. I had made arrangements to pick him up, but when I arrived, no one answered the door. I could see the living room through the window and thought I saw Mr. Nelson there, but when I looked closer, I could see he'd been shot. The front door was unlocked. I let myself in. Of course, my first thought was for his family. I knew he had a wife and kids. So I called out, 'Hello, is anyone home?' something like that— and then I heard the crash."

"That's when Mrs. Nelson drove through the garage?" the reporter confirmed.

"Yes, yes, the sound came from that direction. I ran to see, but the vehicle was already gone. But you can see the ruts."

"Let's get another look at those ruts," the reporter requested, and the screen image shifted again.

"Eric?" Debbi touched his arm. "You don't have to watch this."

"I know." Eric's fingers twitched over the buttons on the remote, but he couldn't bring himself to switch the channel. "They said the kids might be in danger. I have to hear what they think happened."

"It's okay. The forecast can wait. I can look outside. It was warm today, but the evening will be cooler. Typical October in Illinois." Debbi spoke softly, almost as though she was afraid to disturb him.

She'd been that way eight years ago, too, when Vanessa first disappeared, and every time an unexpected memory or a missing-child report would trigger flashbacks. Being here at the cabin where he and Vanessa had spent so much time together both as kids and teens, the memories were closer to the surface, more real and harder to suppress.

Virgil's voice continued as the camera panned in for a close-up of the tire tracks that cut jagged lines through an otherwise picturesque backyard. "What kind of crazy person would drive through the garage wall? And with the kids in the car? At least, I hope she had her kids with her. Who knows what she might have done with them if she did this to Jeff?"

The reporter, instead of shushing the man's musings, encouraged them. "You mentioned you might know what could have prompted her to act, isn't that right, Mr. Greenwood?"

"Oh, Jeff said he thought his wife was having an affair. I suppose she decided to leave him. Maybe they fought about it, I don't know. It's just crazy, isn't it? They need to find those kids before she does anything to them. It's getting dark out."

"And here is a picture of the mother, Madison Nelson, who is believed to have abducted her own children after shooting their father dead." A woman's face appeared on the screen—blond curly hair, tired eyes, a wan smile.

"What kind of crazy woman does a thing like that?" Debbi muttered behind him.

But Eric was too distracted by the image to attempt to answer her question. "She almost looks like Vanessa."

"Vanessa had brown hair, not blond," Debbi corrected quickly. "And she's too young to have a seven-year-old."

"She was seventeen when she disappeared eight years ago."

"She was declared legally dead."

"Doesn't mean she *is* dead."

"Vanessa wouldn't shoot her husband and leave him for another guy."

"That is true. What kind of woman would do a thing like that?" Eric gripped the remote, finally winning the battle to change channels as the reporter intoned about the importance of viewers reporting any sign of the vehicle, the children or their mother—and speculations about the man she may have run away to join. "And what kind of guy would get involved with such a crazy person?"

Sammy was asleep when Vanessa placed his car seat in the concrete manger of the life-size nativity scene in front of her sister's house. She felt a pang of doubt. Was she right to leave the baby with her sister? It was going to be difficult enough to run with the girls. Sammy needed frequent feedings and diaper changes. The girls, at least, could stay quiet when they needed to.

He'd be safer with Alyssa. Wouldn't he? Vanessa looked at the concrete sculptures of Mary and Joseph, poised protectively over the manger. Mary's expression of love and concern seemed to say she'd look over the child.

Vanessa knew she didn't dare linger, no matter how much she wished she could see her sister. If Alyssa saw her, she'd have to take the time to explain, and that would endanger them all. Virgil's men might catch up to her at any time, and Sammy would only be safe if the men who were after her didn't know where she'd left him.

Swallowing back the emotion that tightened her throat and blurred her vision, she ran to the Sequoia, parked almost out of sight down the street. She'd spotted Alyssa going into the house as she pulled up, and suspected, based on the open door to the workshop, her sister would be coming out again soon.

Sure enough, once she was inside the vehicle, she and

the girls watched through the windows as Alyssa stepped outside the front door, headed toward the baby.

Sammy would be safe. Safer, at least, than he would be on the run with her, and that was all that mattered.

Vanessa put the car in gear and drove off into the setting sun. It was dark, and the girls were asleep by the time she turned off the highway to the gravel road that led to the cabin.

She hadn't been there in over eight years, but she'd reviewed the route in her head a hundred thousand times, promising herself that if she ever got a chance to escape, she'd flee to the cabin, the one place she'd never told Jeff about.

Forgotten landmarks leaped into sight like old friends eager to welcome her home as the headlights pierced the night in front of her.

A lump welled up in her throat, but Vanessa swallowed it down. No, she couldn't get emotional, not yet, no matter how many times she'd comforted herself with the hope she might someday see this place again. There was still far too much she had to do.

The Sequoia rolled to a stop in the parking spot in front of the garage. The fishing cabin was just as she remembered it, if a little spooky in the darkness. It was her cabin, or would be someday if her grandfather was still alive. Grandpa had always promised he'd will it to her and her sister.

With a backward glance to be certain the girls were still sleeping peacefully, Vanessa quietly opened the door and hurried to the rock border of the flower bed near the porch. Would the key still be there? Anything could have happened to it in the years since she'd last tucked it away in its hiding spot.

The dim light from the key-chain flashlight barely illuminated the stones, so Vanessa dropped to her knees, feeling each rock in turn, counting them off until she found the correct one. It didn't want to budge, the soil having settled thick around it over the years.

Fighting back panic, Vanessa tugged hard on the rock with both hands, the flashlight beam playing crazily across the cabin until she had the stone rolled onto its side. She regained control of the keychain, aiming the meager light into the dirt.

She saw only bare ground.

"No. It has to be here." She glanced back down the row of rocks, wondering if perhaps she'd chosen the wrong one, but this stone, with its knobby, handgrip-shaped protrusion, was the one. The only one.

She swept her fingers across the dirt, digging lightly, gently.

Something scraped her hand and she stopped, running her index finger along the stiff, buried something, flicking it upward with her fingernail.

The key!

She wiped it clean on her jeans as she rose and bounded up the shallow porch steps to the door. Thankfully, the knob looked familiar, not some new, shiny thing to replace the one that matched the key in her hand. Shaking slightly, it took her a moment to align it with the lock, to slide it inside, wrestle with the knob, hear the click and, finally, with a practiced shove of her hip, pop the door open wide.

Vanessa swiped her hand along the inside of the door frame, found the light switch and flipped it on. Even before her eyes adjusted to the sudden brightness, she saw the man standing across the room at the base of the stairs, facing her from behind the barrel of a gun.

TWO

Eric blinked at the sudden light and tried to get a decent look at the intruder. He wasn't about to hurt anyone—he was pretty sure the old hunting shotgun wasn't even loaded—but Debbi had told him to take it downstairs with him when she'd run to his room in fear after seeing headlights outside. Their cabin was deep on private property. No one else ought to be there, certainly not in the middle of the night.

Still half-asleep, his mind muddled by dreams tainted with the memories unearthed by that evening's news story, he couldn't help wondering if he was actually awake.

The face staring back at him from the doorway was the same one from his dreams, the same one from the newscast, familiar but completely impossible.

"Eric?"

He nodded, swallowed, couldn't say the name that rose to his lips.

Vanessa was dead. Legally dead.

"Can you put the gun down?" The woman spoke with Vanessa's voice, which for all the years that had passed was still the same, maybe a little tired, even frantic.

He lowered the hunting shotgun but didn't let go. More awake now—quite shocked awake—he realized a number of things all at once.

This *was* the woman from the picture on the news, the woman who'd killed her husband just before dinnertime in a quiet Chicago suburb. She was dangerous. Her children were in danger. The reporter had called her Madison Nelson.

Should he let on that he knew who she was?

And why did she remind him so much of Vanessa, who was supposed to be dead? What was she doing here, in the cabin where he and Vanessa had spent so many happy times as children and teens?

Before he could sort it out, a voice echoed from outside the house.

"Mommy?"

The woman darted back out of the cabin.

Still unsure what was going on, Eric nonetheless realized the voice he'd heard probably belonged to one of Madison Nelson's daughters—what were their names?

"It's okay, Abby."

Eric remembered the moment he overheard the woman soothing her daughter. Abby and Emma. And Sammy.

Abby had clambered half out of the Toyota Sequoia—the same vehicle featured in the news broadcast. Eric couldn't see in the darkness, but he felt certain the front of the vehicle was probably banged up, at least a bit.

Abby clung to her mother, and the woman stroked her hair and held her close. "I'm right here. Mommy's right here, honey. We're at the place I told you about—the cabin."

"The most wonderful place in the world?"

"That's the one. It will look more welcoming once the sun rises. Let's get you into bed."

"With the kitten quilt? Did you find the kitten quilt?"

"I didn't have time to look. We'll see. Can you walk? I need to carry your sister."

Eric listened, still unsure whether he was dreaming or

what exactly was going on. The woman sounded like a loving parent, but weren't most psychotic killers supposed to seem normal on the outside? More disturbing still, Eric felt sure that somehow, though this woman matched the description of Madison Nelson, she was Vanessa, who was supposed to be dead.

After all, she had a key to the cabin, and she knew about the kitten quilt.

Abby slid down from the high SUV and blinked up at him warily. "Who's that?"

Eric looked at the woman—Vanessa? Could it be Vanessa? Or was she Madison now?

She cast him a brief, uncertain glance. "That's my friend Eric. He's okay."

Something welled up inside him at the words and the reassurance that filled the little girl's face. Even the girl looked a lot like Vanessa had looked when they were kids together, playing in the yard here at the cabin, chasing fireflies after dark.

What had happened? Eight years ago, one of his best friends had disappeared, and now this woman was here, knowing things Vanessa would know—acting and talking like Vanessa, even looking like her, aside from the blond hair and eight years of passing time.

When the little girl stumbled uncertainly after her mother, Eric held out his hand.

Abby looked up at him with eyes so much like Vanessa's had been at that age, he couldn't speak. But the little girl trustingly placed her hand in his, and he steadied her as they walked into the cabin.

"Debbi and I have the upstairs bedrooms," Eric explained as they entered, as though this was a regular, planned visit, and he hadn't just been pointing a gun at the woman.

"The downstairs bedroom just has one bed—"

"It's a bunk bed now, the kind with a single on top and double below. Some buddies of mine sold it after college. I thought the cabin could use it."

"Perfect. This way, girls."

Eric let go of Abby's hand as her mother led her toward the bedroom. Still not quite certain he wasn't dreaming, he tried to assure himself he wasn't doing anything illegal by offering hospitality to a murderer—after all, he didn't know for a fact she'd murdered anyone, did he? Maybe it was self-defense? Maybe a lot of things had happened in the past eight years. All he knew was that he'd prayed for years that his friend would be safe, and now all of a sudden, here she was with little girls who needed a helping hand.

He wasn't about to turn them away. Besides, even if she was a psychotic murderer, he ought to make sure her kids were safe. Shouldn't he?

Eric bounded up the stairs to fetch the kitten quilt, which was usually kept folded at the foot of the bed in Debbi's room. The beloved blanket from their childhood had come with the cabin, and even though it was a little juvenile for his twenty-five-year-old sister, it was too soft and delightful to get put away in a closet, unused.

His sister peeked at him from the doorway as he approached her room.

"It's the Toyota Sequoia—I shined my high-beam flashlight out the window. The license plate matches the one on the news." She followed him into her room, where her laptop sat on the end of the bed, open to a news page about the missing children and their murdering mother. "That's Madison Nelson, isn't it?"

"Shh. If it is, do you want her to know you know who she is?"

Debbi's eyes widened, and she clamped her mouth shut.

"Something's going on." Eric lifted the laptop, pulled the kitten quilt out from underneath it and explained briefly, "I'm nearly positive that's Vanessa Jackson downstairs."

"Eric, no." Debbi's voice fell into the chiding tone she'd used long before when he'd vowed to go out searching one more time. "She's been declared—"

"I know." Eric didn't want to hear the words again. "But nobody ever found out what happened to her. All I know is, Vanessa was my friend. I've got to help my friend."

Debbi grabbed his arm as he stepped toward the bedroom door. "Even if it means aiding a known criminal?" She showed him the cell phone she held in her hand. "I was about to call the police."

Eric sucked in a breath, his conscience in sudden conflict. Any other time, he'd say it was the right thing to do. "If Vanessa wanted to go to the police, she'd have done it already."

"So we let her kill us in our sleep?"

"She's not going to hurt us. Not in front of her kids." He'd seen enough of the way the woman interacted with the girls to know she was purposely protecting them. That she was used to protecting them. But how far had she gone to protect them?

Debbi cut off his thoughts. "That didn't stop her from killing her husband."

"We don't know what happened." Eric wasn't sure he wanted to know, exactly. He could guess at a few things, but all of them involved the kind of ugliness and hurt he wouldn't wish on anyone, certainly not on the girl he'd cared for so strongly. "We should at least wait and hear her story. Can you wait that long?"

"How long will that be?"

"Give me an hour, maybe two. If she won't tell us what's going on, then you can call the police."

"Fine." Debbi flashed him the look she always gave him when he outfished or outmaneuvered her. Her final words floated after him on a sigh as he headed back down the stairs. "Although I don't see why she'd let us live once we know what she's up to."

"Mommy, the kitten quilt."

"I'm going to look for it."

"No, it's there." Abby pointed.

Vanessa turned to see Eric standing in the doorway, an uncertain look on his face, kitten quilt in hand. "Ah. Thank you." She accepted the quilt, which solved one tiny problem while introducing various others.

Her first priority from the moment the shadow of Virgil's Land Rover had darkened the basement walls had been to get her girls tucked safely into bed at this cabin. But she hadn't expected anyone to be there, certainly not Eric, the friend she'd long ago wished would be more than a friend, whose presence complicated everything. She felt a stab of guilt as she avoided looking him in the eye, instead focusing her attention on tucking the quilt securely around her daughters on the double-size lower bunk.

"Good night, Mommy." Abby and Emma effectively dismissed her, snuggling in under the blanket as though they were on one of the countless innocent visits she and her sister had made to the cabin a generation before. She'd prayed for something like this for them—but not this way, not going through what they'd been through, or what yet lay ahead.

"Good night." There was nothing more to do or say. She couldn't put off facing Eric any longer.

She closed the door behind her and stepped toward the living room, deciding as she did so to ask questions first, to play offense instead of defense and maybe put off answering too many questions until she knew a bit more about what was going on.

Eric stood in the middle of the cabin's great room, near

the table that separated the open kitchen from the sofa and television on the other side.

She glanced at him only briefly, saw confusion and maybe even anger on his face, and quickly looked away, taking in all that had changed and all that had stayed the same in the cabin. Her grandmother's knitted afghan still topped the sofa, but it was a newer sofa. Some of the pictures on the walls were the same. Some had changed. The familiarity of it all made her want to sob with relief, but she held herself together. She had to. For the kids.

"So, you—" Eric started.

Vanessa remembered her plan and cut off his question quickly. "What are you doing here?"

"It's my place."

"No, it's not. It's mine."

"Alyssa sold it to me."

"So my grandfather—"

"He died. Six years ago."

She'd told herself that much was likely. Her grandfather was old, and his health had been declining rapidly, but the words still hit her like one of Jeff's controlling blows.

And just like in the early days when Jeff hit her, Vanessa fought back. "So Alyssa sold you her half? Half the cabin was supposed to go to me."

"Your sister sold me both halves."

"She can't sell my half—"

"She can. You were declared legally dead." Eric took a step toward her. "What's going on, Vanessa? Or should I call you Madison?"

Vanessa pinched her eyes shut at the words, which struck her like another blow. "How do you know—"

"It was on the news."

"What was?"

Eric opened his mouth, looked toward the ceiling and made a resigned noise in his throat. "Maybe you should just watch it yourself. I can find it online. But first—what happened to the baby? Sammy? He wasn't in the vehicle."

Vanessa heard real concern, maybe even fear in Eric's voice, almost enough to drown out her own terror over what the news might have to say. "I left him with my sister."

"Alyssa knows you're alive, then?"

Much as she'd have liked to confirm his words, she knew it wouldn't be entirely honest to do so. "She'll figure it out. I need to see that newscast."

"I'll be right back."

Eric climbed the steps and returned with a laptop, which he set on the table. The website was already up on the screen.

"Debbi had it open," he explained quietly as the broadcast began to play.

Vanessa reached past him to adjust the volume, just loud enough for her to hear without risking the girls overhearing anything from the other side of the bedroom door. She'd made too many sacrifices to preserve their innocence, to let it be destroyed now.

"Authorities are asking everyone in the Chicago region to be on the lookout for this vehicle, driven by Madison Nelson of Barrington, who is believed to have shot her husband dead before driving through the back wall of their garage with their three children in the vehicle."

"Dead," Vanessa repeated softly. She'd expected it from the moment the Land Rover pulled into the driveway. Still, hearing the words, seeing the images of the house where she'd been held captive for so long, made her tremble.

Pictures flashed across the screen—her home, the prison where she'd been held, surrounded by yellow police tape. The broken-out back wall of her garage. The vehicle, which was now parked outside. Pictures of her children and a particularly unflattering photograph of her, which had been taken mere minutes after she'd given birth to Sammy after a grueling labor.

But the most horrifying thing wasn't the pictures. It wasn't even the fact that Jeff was dead.

"They think *I* killed him? Why would they think that?"

No sooner had she voiced the question than Virgil appeared on the screen, saying horrible things about her, voicing ugly motives made all the more terrifying because, to anyone who didn't know her, they would sound plausible. And no one really knew her, not anymore. So everyone would think Virgil's lies were true.

"You didn't kill him?" Eric's voice behind her was soft, even cautious.

She turned and met his eyes for the first time. "No, I most certainly did not."

Eric looked visibly relieved.

Vanessa might have felt offended that he'd doubted her, except that, given what she'd seen on the news broadcast, he had every right to believe the worst. Gratitude welled up inside her that he was willing to trust her word over that of everyone else. She pulled out a chair and sat down, the weight of the news broadcast too much to bear standing up.

She needed to explain a few things quickly. "He kidnapped me. He hid me and gave me that name, made me dye my hair, broke my nose once and it healed with a bump."

Eric nodded patiently. "So, who killed him?"

"He did—" she pointed at Virgil, who was still on the screen "—or one of the guys who works for him."

For a long, silent moment, Vanessa looked at Eric, waiting for some sign that would indicate whether he believed her or not. She wasn't sure what she would do if he didn't. All she knew was that she had to keep her children safe. The news report was a terrifying development. Where could she go without being recognized? Where could she hide?

Finally, Eric spoke. "Can you prove these guys killed him?"

Vanessa blinked, her shock at being free, her uncertainty about what to do next, clouding her thoughts, muddling her judgment.

"Look, Vanessa, I want to help you, but this does not look good. Debbi wants to call the police."

"No! Don't do that. Please." Vanessa wrapped her arms around her shoulders, wishing for the millionth time that none of this had ever happened. She'd gotten away, but only briefly. Her face was all over the news. She'd have to stay in hiding, keep her daughters in hiding, or she'd go to jail and lose her kids. "If you call the police, they'll take the kids. I'll go to jail, their word against mine." She repeated the threat Jeff had ingrained in her, the fear that had kept her frozen in the basement, even when she thought about breaking out a window and running for help.

"What happened, Vanessa? You disappeared eight years ago, and everybody thought you were dead. What's been going on?"

"It's a trafficking ring. They're criminals."

"Who are? This Virgil guy?"

"And Jeff—they came to the house and killed Jeff this evening. I ran with the kids or they would have killed us, too." She swallowed, hating the words, hating the memories. "Jeff kidnapped me eight years ago as part of this human-trafficking scheme. They take girls and traffic them, but Jeff kept me to himself. He left me tied up when he wasn't around until Abby was born.

"Once Abby was born, he allowed me just enough freedom to take care of her, never enough to get away from him. He was always there, for every minute of every medical appointment, every second I was ever around other people, watching me, making sure I didn't reach out for help. Not like I would try anything—I knew he'd go after my family if I did or take Abby from me. It's a big ugly crime ring. They run drugs, too. They use the drugs to control people. Virgil's just one piece of it."

Eric swallowed slowly, as if forcing himself to digest her words. "Can you prove it?"

"I know a few things, but no, I don't have any evidence against them. Any time I saw a piece of paper I wasn't supposed to see, Jeff warned me what would happen if I ever so much as touched anything that could be used as evidence against them. I purposely closed my eyes. I had no choice."

"The only way to prove your innocence is to prove these guys are guilty."

"I agree." Vanessa nodded. But at the same time, Eric's words scared her. "But Virgil's not the ringleader. He was Jeff's contact, some kind of bully employed to keep guys like Jeff in line, but he wasn't in charge. If we turn in Virgil, that's just cutting off an arm."

"And the real monster would turn on you," Eric muttered, understanding. "So, who's the ringleader? We find him, find evidence against him, and we can prove your innocence."

Vanessa liked the idea. If they could shut down the trafficking ring, all the other innocent girls who'd been taken just like her could go free.

There was just one problem.

"I don't know who's in charge."

THREE

Eric was wide-awake now, but he almost wished he could roll over and forget this nightmare had ever happened. Except that Vanessa was back. He'd prayed for her safe return, even imagined himself holding her tight if he ever had the chance again. But the fact that she was a wanted fugitive gave him pause. He wanted to believe she was innocent, but there were too many things he didn't understand.

"Want to tell me what happened? Maybe we can sort out how to catch this guy, or what to do, or something." Eric was also hoping that he'd learn enough to tell him whether he was crazy for trusting Vanessa. He wanted to pull her into his arms, to embrace her as he'd always pictured himself embracing her if she was ever found. But if she'd been held captive by a man for eight years, maybe she wouldn't welcome his touch. He held back, waiting for some sign from her that would tell him if it would be okay for him to reach out to her.

"Oh, wow, where do I start?"

"How about the night you went missing?"

Vanessa closed her eyes, gulped a breath and then shook her head. "I need to start before that. You know I was working as a waitress at the Flaming Pheasant down by the interstate."

"That's where you were last seen, getting off work at

the end of your shift. You walked out the back door, but you never came home. Your car was still in the spot where you parked it when you arrived at work." Eric filled in what he knew.

Vanessa nodded, confirming his words. "There was a guy, the same man who was murdered this evening. Back then he was young and handsome and charming. He was a regular at the restaurant. He'd say the kindest things to me. 'You have pretty eyes' or 'I like your smile'—not creepy things or even really hitting on me. I just thought he was nice, you know. Unlike a lot of other customers, he never complained, never got impatient when the kitchen was slow. The restaurant often wasn't busy, so we'd chat. It got to where I looked forward to seeing him. My day was better if he showed up."

Eric felt a bead of cold sweat creeping down his arm as Vanessa spoke. If he hadn't known where her story was going, it would have sounded so innocent. He might have felt jealous of the guy, but he wouldn't have been suspicious.

"Slowly, he started to learn things about me. Asked where I was from, about my family. I told him that I lived with my grandfather, about how my parents died in a car crash when Alyssa and I were little—told him I had a twin sister. Maybe I should have been suspicious that he was interested to hear about me, but he was always so friendly and positive about everything, I couldn't resist talking to him."

Much as Eric wished Vanessa would hurry with her story, or even skip over the parts that made his skin crawl, nonetheless, he sensed it was important for him to hear it. Not just in case there were details that might help them track down the leader of the trafficking ring, but because, after all, Vanessa had been through a terrible trauma. She needed to tell someone what had happened.

He also felt strongly the need to hear her out. Eight years ago, he'd failed her. He hadn't been there for her. But he was here now. He had a second chance—the kind of second chance he'd prayed for, but never really dared to dream he might get. He could be here for her now. It wouldn't change the past, but it was the best he could do.

Vanessa looked down at her hands as she spoke, as though eye contact would be too difficult, given the content of her story. "Then one weekend, I was really bummed that I had to work, because I wanted to come out here to the cabin. Jeff said he wanted to make me feel better, that he wanted to do something special. He offered to take me out after I got off work. By then I felt like I knew him, even though I didn't, really."

Eric didn't want to interrupt, but he had to. "You didn't tell him about the cabin, did you?" If Jeff knew about the cabin, then he might have told Virgil or any of their associates. They could track them down. No doubt they wouldn't want someone at large who knew so much about them. They were probably looking for Vanessa right now, not content to let the police and television viewers do their searching for them.

"No. I never told him about this place. It's too special to me. It didn't feel right to share it with him, even before..." Her voice trailed off.

"So you went out with him after work?" Eric prompted, dreading to hear what came next.

"Yes. I got in his car, and at first he was just as charming as ever. But we didn't stop. He kept driving toward Chicago, and I realized I didn't know where I was and didn't know where he was taking me or how to get home again. It was dark out, almost winter, and very cold. I started to ask questions, and he just kept assuring me that he had a special place in mind, and I was going to love it." Her voice broke.

"I didn't love it. I hated it," she whispered, shaking her head, her unspoken words telling him vastly more of the horrors she'd suffered than anything she might have said. "He tied me up, did whatever he wanted to me." She wiped away a tear, gulped a breath and kept talking.

"He kept me tied up for nearly a year. When I got pregnant with Abby, for a long time he threatened me that I wouldn't be able to keep her, but eventually he came around and took me to the doctor for medical care, but only once I promised not to let on about who I really was. He had these fake IDs. I was Madison Nelson, supposedly four years older than I really am, with blond hair. After that, he didn't keep me tied up, just locked in the basement with my baby.

"For a long time, I tried to think of a way to escape, to get away when he wasn't looking, but I couldn't leave Abby behind, and I couldn't run with a baby. Once I got pregnant with Emma, I knew there was no way. I hadn't been able to escape with one child—how could I run away with two? So I turned my attention from thinking about how to escape, to thinking about how to give my girls something resembling a normal life. Jeff recognized the change and let us out more, even took us to the park, but he was always there with his gun on him when I wasn't locked away."

Eric wasn't sure what to do or say. Part of him wanted to pull her into his arms, to hold her tight enough to squeeze the brokenness inside her back together. But he didn't dare do that. The fact that she couldn't even look at him told him she wasn't ready to welcome his embrace.

Back when they were high-school friends, he'd more than once worked up the courage to place his hand on her back or his arm across her shoulder, innocent ways of testing whether she felt anything for him like what he felt for her. But he'd never gotten a clear indication from her either way, and after all she'd been through, he wasn't sure how she'd respond to the old gestures of their friendship. As a high-school science teacher, he didn't play a huge role in helping those who'd been abused, but he'd had some training on how to spot signs of abuse and what to do about it. So he kept his hands to himself and listened as she continued her story.

"Jeff used the kids for leverage. And I think maybe that's why he got sucked into work so much—his boss used the kids for leverage, too. That's how I knew I needed to be ready to leave. I overheard Virgil's threats the last time. He wanted money—I don't know how much, but I know it was a lot, more than we had, which supposedly Jeff had kept back from some of the deals he'd run, or that he'd missed out on by not running some deals, I don't know. They wanted the money, or they were going to kill us. All five of us."

At her words, Eric remembered. "Your son, Sammy. You said you left him with your sister, but she doesn't even know you're alive?"

"I wrote a note on the shirt he was wearing. It said 'A DNA test will prove this is Alyssa Jackson's son.' It wasn't a lie," she clarified. "Sammy isn't Alyssa's son, obviously, but since we're identical twins, a DNA test would still conclude she's his mother."

"So, you handed him to her?"

"No. I couldn't risk that—I couldn't let her see me or she'd come looking for me, and that might lead Virgil to her. That's the same reason I didn't use Sammy's name. No, I left him in her manger."

"In her manger? The nativity scene? Her concrete sculptures?"

"Yes. The nativity scene is up next to the house. I watched her working in the yard, saw her go inside the house, and I left him in his car seat in the manger with his diaper bag. Then I drove away a couple of blocks and watched until she went outside and saw him."

For all of Eric's fears that Vanessa might be crazy, leaving her son in a manger was nearly enough to convince him. Granted, the weather that day was warm for October. The baby would be fine outside, even if he wasn't noticed for a couple hours or more. And she had stood by to make sure her sister found him.

"But why did you leave him with her?"

Vanessa looked him full in the face, her warm brown eyes boring into his. "To keep him safe. I don't believe, even for a second, that Virgil or the people he works for are going to let me get away easily. They'll look for me. They're probably trying to track me down right now. They know I know what happened. If the cops find me first, I'll go to jail and lose my girls. If the traffickers find me..." She shook her head. "I thought about leaving the girls with Alyssa, too. I debated where they'd be safest. But if three kids go missing and then three suddenly appear somewhere else, that might lead Virgil to them. And he knows the girls are old enough to identify him. No, this way, we're split up. If something happens to me, at least Sammy has a chance."

Her voice broke again, and Eric realized how difficult the decision must have been—to choose to leave her son with her sister, as a gamble that one way or another, at least part of her family might escape the criminals who had terrorized them for the past eight years.

But even more than the pain of her story, Eric felt chilled by the threat that had led her to abandon her infant son. "Do you really think they're trying to track you down right now?"

"I'm sure of it." Vanessa shuddered. "They've always made it a point to make an example of those who disobey them. In fact, that's where they got my identity. The real

Madison tried to run. They tracked her down, left her body in a shallow grave and made me look like the picture on her driver's license. Jeff forced me to marry him, and that got me a new ID with his last name. Nobody ever questioned, because she hadn't been reported missing yet. She wasn't a minor."

"You're sure they don't know about the cabin?" Eric clarified.

"I wouldn't have come here if they did." Vanessa sucked in a breath and covered her mouth with her hand. "Oh, no!"

"What is it?" Eric leaned over the chair where she sat.

Vanessa fought to keep calm, but the events of the day were catching up to her, and the latest realization was too much to bear. She'd been so focused on getting the girls to the cabin without being recognized, on making sure they got to sleep peacefully and then explaining her story to Eric, she hadn't thought about the fact that now seemed so painfully obvious.

"I have to leave."

"Leave here? Now?"

"As soon as possible. I can't stay here. I'm sorry—I didn't think. I mean, I thought this was my place—mine and Alyssa's, anyway. It didn't occur to me she might have sold it."

"She needed the money to keep her concrete-sculpture business going. I was helping her out, in a way. And of course, I always loved it when your grandfather invited my grandpa and me here for fishing trips." Eric looked a bit confused at Vanessa's alarm.

She hurried to explain. "But they're looking for me. If they track me here—that drags you into this. I can't let them know about you. It puts you in danger. I have to go." She stood.

"You're not going anywhere right now." Eric placed a

hand on her shoulder, not pushing down, really, but enough to guide her back into the chair. "Your girls are asleep—are you thinking of leaving without them?"

"Of course not."

"Don't you need your sleep?"

"I can't sleep, not with all that's happened and everything I have to think about."

Eric pinched the bridge of his nose, a gesture Vanessa hadn't witnessed in years, which she nonetheless immediately recognized as his thinking face. She watched him, waiting for him to announce whatever it was he was thinking about, grateful for the light touch of his hand on her shoulder.

Even as she waited, she couldn't help noticing how much he'd changed in the years they'd been apart. She'd recognized him immediately, but only because he was a familiar part of her memories of the cabin—her grandfather and his grandfather had been inseparable fishing buddies and equally devoted to their grandchildren. So in many ways, though she hadn't at all expected to see him there, he still fit, in spite of the gun he'd been holding.

On closer inspection now, she saw the differences. He was taller, broader through the shoulders, the stubble on his chin deeply shadowed by this hour. He'd be twenty-five, as well, the same age she really was, though her Madison Nelson ID had her at twenty-nine. His dark hair hadn't thinned, and his dark brown eyes still sparkled like obsidian beneath brows that had thickened with age.

He looked good, as familiar as home and yet fascinatingly different from the boy she'd known. She'd thought about him often during the long, lonely hours of her captivity, but her memories couldn't compete with being in his presence. She wanted to turn into the arm that was draped so lightly across her shoulder, to bury her face against his chest and sob for all she'd lost and all she might still lose, but she felt afraid to. Probably post-traumatic inhibition, but it stayed her hand.

"Can we," Eric spoke slowly, releasing his nose and meeting her eyes, "*try* to find out who's behind this trafficking ring? If we can't go to the police and we can't stay here for long, really, the only way I can see out of this is to slay the dragon, to cut off its head."

Vanessa recognized the phrase from the game they'd played countless times in the woods around the cabin. A gnarled stump of a tree had been their dragon, its branches hooked like claws, dark and menacing. As kids, they'd hacked at it with their "swords" made of sticks.

"They left it dead, and with its head they went galumphing back." Vanessa paraphrased the line from Lewis Carroll's "Jabberwocky," the poetry bringing back a flood of forgotten dreams. They'd both been going to be high-school teachers, he in science, she in English. Their dreams had been so bright before Jeff had extinguished them.

"Can we?" Eric asked again after a long pause.

Reluctantly, Vanessa stopped remembering those old dreams and instead focused on the nightmare she was living. How could they possibly track down the criminals when she didn't know who was really behind everything? Jeff would have known, though he'd never said a word in eight long years. But Jeff was dead now. She didn't have any way of accessing—

She stood abruptly.

"What?" Eric looked startled but hopeful.

Vanessa ran back outside and pulled the keys from where she'd left them in the Sequoia's ignition. Besides the chip that started the SUV, there were half a dozen other traditional keys, plus a couple of smaller ones that looked as if they might go to a file cabinet or desk drawer.

Eric waited on the porch, watching her as she ran back, examining the keys.

"I took Jeff's keys."

"What do the keys go to?"

"Lots of things. His office building, his office—these look like they might open some files. I know he had files, incriminating files. He was extremely protective of them whenever he had to bring some home. He never wanted me to touch them." She paused on the porch, holding the keys between them, and looked into his face, awaiting his verdict, wondering what he would think of her idea. Jeff always hated her ideas, hated that she ever thought for herself, but Eric wasn't Jeff. "Those files would expose Jeff. We might even learn who the real head of the monster is."

"Do you know where Jeff's office is?"

"Yes. I've been inside the building several times when he needed to run in for something. Assuming he still works in the same place, I can find it again. I made it a point to remember, if only because I knew he didn't want me to."

"Good for you." Eric gave her half a smile.

"So, you think it's a good idea?"

"To let you walk into the dragon's lair?"

"How else am I going to cut off its head?" She met his eyes, challenging him, hopeful for the very first time. Could she really find and destroy the head of the crime ring that had ruined her life? If it was possible, she'd do whatever she had to do. It was either that or spend the rest of her life hiding in fear.

"You're not going." Eric shook his head, everything on his face saying he thought she was crazy. Then he finished, "Not alone, not without someone to stand guard, to watch out for you. And you're definitely not taking your kids. They can stay here with Debbi. We can't take your Sequoia—it's all over the news. We'll hide it in the garage and take my car, but we need to do it tonight, while it's still dark, before they have a chance to realize we might come looking and destroy the evidence before we get there. I'll drive."

Hope surged inside her, and Vanessa's arms flew up, ready to hug Eric for agreeing with her plan—for wanting to be a part of it, even. But she caught herself just in time, and instead she gripped the keys harder and turned, following him back into the cabin.

"Stop right there," Debbi ordered as they entered.

Vanessa looked up to see Eric's sister, now in her early twenties, dropping a pair of buckshot shells into the hunting shotgun Eric had been holding earlier.

Debbi clicked the barrel into place and stared them down. "Neither of you is going anywhere. I'm calling the police."

FOUR

"Debbi, no." Eric addressed his sister in a calming tone. She wouldn't shoot. She didn't even like hunting. The gun shook in her trembling hands. He'd known she was terrified about having Vanessa at the cabin, but he'd hoped she'd give him a little more time before her fears caught up to her.

"Harboring a criminal is illegal." Debbi's voice wavered unsteadily. "We could go to prison because of her."

"She didn't kill her husband," Eric explained.

"I didn't," Vanessa echoed.

Eric continued, moving slowly closer to his sister. "He wasn't even her husband—legally, maybe, but not in the traditional sense of the word. He kidnapped her. She's the victim of a human-trafficking ring. We have to help her."

Debbi gripped the gun with both hands. "The police can help her."

"No," Vanessa pleaded with the same note of panic Eric had heard in her voice when he'd mentioned the police before. "The guys who killed Jeff are professionals. While I'm trying to convince the police to believe me, these guys will cover their tracks so thick the police will never find them. But they'll find me and get their revenge."

"Debbi, please." Eric piggybacked on Vanessa's words. "Vanessa has keys to her kidnapper's office. We can go tonight and get evidence to put these guys away for good. But we have to go now, before they catch up to her."

Debbi narrowed her eyes warily but lowered the gun a few inches. "Once you get the evidence, we can call the police?"

Eric looked to Vanessa for the answer.

"Yes. Once we have evidence against these guys, we'll call the police. We can go and be back in a matter of hours if we leave now."

"Please, Debbi?" Eric reasoned with his sister, praying she'd understand, or at least give them a chance to prove Vanessa's innocence. His sister was scared, that was all. Normally, she was a very kind person.

Debbi shifted her weight, planting the gun against the floor like a walking stick, leaning against it as she eyed them conspiratorially. "Fine." She blew out a breath that said she might still regret caving. "What's our plan?"

Together, they quickly assembled everything they'd need. Eric wasn't surprised, given Vanessa's story, to hear she didn't have a cell phone. Eight years before, she'd been too poor to afford a phone of her own.

"I'll stand guard outside while you go in the building," Eric decided. "But I'll need some way to contact you if someone's coming."

Debbi pulled her phone from her purse. "She can take mine. Nobody ever calls or texts me in the middle of the night."

"But what if *we* need to reach you? The cabin's never had a landline. We don't have any other phones."

"You're going to stand watch while she goes inside, right?" Debbi clarified. "You're going to need a phone to call her while she's inside, or there's no point in you standing watch. Who do you think needs it more?"

Vanessa blew out a thoughtful breath, then spoke slowly. "I brought the girls here to keep them safe. I don't have a phone. I didn't figure we'd have a phone. So leaving them here with Debbi isn't really any different than being here myself, without a phone."

"It might be risky going inside the office. Riskier than staying here." Eric accepted the device from his sister and passed it to Vanessa. "I'll text you if someone's coming. Do you know how to answer a text on this phone?" He sent a text between the phones so she could see how it worked.

"Got it."

"If this thing goes off, you'll need to get out of sight." His fingers brushed hers as he spoke, imparting an acute sense of awareness.

Vanessa's glance fluttered from his fingers to his eyes and back again. Her cheeks colored slightly as she thanked him and agreed to his plan.

So she'd felt it, too, then. The old chemistry, the teenager-like nervousness he'd thought he'd lost the night she never came home. He'd been crazy for her for years, but equally terrified she'd find out how he felt. He'd never told her, never let on to his feelings…and regretted it ever since. He'd prayed for a second chance.…

A surge of emotion welled inside him, but he swallowed quickly, pushing it back before it could creep into his voice. "Okay, then, I think we're ready. You've got your key-chain flashlight. Debbi will stay here with the girls—"

"They should sleep until after I get back," Vanessa predicted. "They won't ever know I was gone."

Eric nodded, not trusting his voice anymore, the reference to her absence too much, the reality of her presence slowly eclipsing his surprise. She was alive, she was here. She looked great, but she'd been through so many awful experiences, scars buried deeper than he could see. He wanted to throw his arms open wide and embrace her, but he was terrified of how she might respond.

Debbi insisted he take the hunting shotgun and a box

of buckshot. While Vanessa hastily left instructions for what Debbi should do if the girls awoke before they returned, Eric carried the gun outside and put it in his car. He hoped he wouldn't need it, but these men had killed a man today already. He had to be prepared for the worst. They couldn't hurt Vanessa, not again, not if he had any say in the matter.

He couldn't think of anything else to bring, but moved the Sequoia out of the way, backed his Mustang out of the garage and then parked the wanted SUV out of sight inside.

By the time he pulled the garage door closed, Vanessa stood by his car, ready to go.

How many times had he wished for such a simple thing, to see her standing by his car, leaving with him? They'd never gone out on a proper date. He'd been too nervous to ask, and then it was too late.

At least tonight, he was able to open the door for her. Their eyes met briefly as she stepped past him and took a seat inside the vehicle.

In spite of the darkness of the northern Illinois woods at night, he could see the fear clearly on her face. Unsure what he could possibly say to reassure her, he closed her door, then climbed in behind the wheel.

"You'll have to tell me how to find this place," he reminded her as he navigated the twisting gravel driveway.

"Just get on highway fourteen and follow it toward Chicago for a while." She fell silent then.

Eric had hoped to chat, but he wasn't sure what to say. He couldn't commiserate with her because he didn't know all about what she'd been through, nor did he feel comfortable asking, certainly not now. Perhaps they ought to discuss what lay ahead, but everything depended upon what she would find in Jeff's office.

After a long silence, Vanessa spoke in a quiet voice.

"Thank you." Her voice hitched, as though she was about to say more, but had to fight back a sob.

Eric hesitated to respond, listening for whatever she'd been about to say, reluctant to speak for fear he might cut her off. They drove in silence awhile longer. Finally, he offered, "It's no problem."

She made a sound that was half laughter, half miserable sigh. "Yes, it is. You could get in big trouble for helping me. Debbi probably had the right idea. You might regret that you didn't listen to her."

"Never," he vowed quickly.

Vanessa glanced at him, and he took his eyes off the road just long enough to meet her eyes.

"My only regret is that I didn't do something eight years ago."

"Do what?"

"I don't know. Something, so that you wouldn't ever have disappeared."

"There's nothing you could have done. You didn't know. I didn't know."

"But you were vulnerable. I mean, that Jeff guy, he preyed on you. It shouldn't have happened. How could something like that happen? To you, of all people? I mean, I know you're beautiful—"

"I don't think so." Vanessa cut him off, her tone outwardly joking, sarcastic with an undertone of longing so buried, he might have thought he'd imagined it.

But he couldn't let her believe otherwise. "Vanessa, you are. You're beautiful, and that's why he targeted you."

"You don't know why he picked me. How could you know? You never met him."

"I know you. And I know—" He squeezed the steering wheel, wishing he'd spoken these words long before. Would it have made any difference? He was speaking them now. "I know he saw what I saw, which was a girl whose smile could make everything else bad that had happened that day disappear. A girl whose smile you want to see every day of your life. But instead of treasuring you, he *took* you."

"Watch the road," Vanessa cautioned.

Eric realized he'd gotten so caught up in his words, he'd veered onto the shoulder of the dark highway. He realigned the vehicle with the path. "Sorry. I just— I've regretted it all these years, and now you're here, but these guys might show up again or the police could take you away anytime. But you have to know." He realized his words were rambling. Words had always been Vanessa's area of expertise, never his. "I should have said it long ago, but I was so awed by you. I wanted to ask you out, but I was afraid you'd laugh at me."

"I would never laugh at you."

"Oh, yeah, never?" He quoted, "'He'd a French cocked-hat on his forehead, a bunch of lace at his chin—'"

"I wasn't laughing *at* you. I was laughing *with* you."

"I wasn't laughing." Eric remembered vividly his attempt to play out Alfred Noyes's infamous poem, "The Highwayman," for the girl who'd loved it so. Admittedly, he'd looked ridiculous, his French cocked-hat, a pirate tricorn, the bunch of lace at his chin a borrowed blouse of Debbi's. But he'd wanted so much to impress Vanessa.

"The turn is coming up, just past the railroad tracks."

Eric turned his attention to the road and tried to forget his disastrous attempt at demonstrating his affection without actually saying how he'd felt.

Now he thought Vanessa was going to forget, as well, but she offered softly, "I didn't know how to respond. I was so flattered that you dressed up in costume and everything. It was either giggle like an idiot or admit that I was blown away."

"Blown away?"

"This next corner, at the stoplight. Turn right, then right again on the access road."

Eric followed her instructions, wishing he'd chosen to hold the conversation at a time when they could actually talk. But they'd held off in silence for too much of the ride, and now it was too late. Again.

"Here it is, this office building."

"This is it? Is this the crime-ring headquarters, or did Jeff do honest work, too?"

"Jeff never did any honest work. Hmm, you'll want to park somewhere you can't be seen."

Eric pulled past the building, all the parking places out in the open. "Here, behind this Dumpster?" He turned past a few thick cedar trees that divided the lots, then came to a stop.

Vanessa glanced around. "This looks like as good a spot as any." She opened the car door, then glanced back.

"Are you sure you don't want me to go in instead? It's so risky. If there's anybody in there—"

"There aren't any cars around, so I doubt anyone is inside. Besides, you don't know your way around like I do. I'll find it faster. That makes it less risky if I go in."

Eric hung his head. Vanessa was right—he just felt terrible that he couldn't do more for her. "Got everything you need?" he asked, not ready for her to walk away, not yet, when so much between them was still unsaid.

She looked down at the bundle of keys in her hand and patted the pocket that held Debbi's phone, set to vibrate. "The sun will be up in a matter of hours. People could start arriving anytime. With Jeff dead—well, they might have the same thought I had, that his office could hold evidence. I should hurry."

Eric reached over and gave her hand a quick squeeze, but she was already climbing out of the car. Did he imagine that she squeezed his hand in return, or was that just wishful thinking?

Vanessa darted toward the building without looking back.

In spite of the number of keys on the ring, Vanessa was able to find the correct one quickly. She entered the building, glanced around the large open foyer and ascended the staircase. Jeff had always left her downstairs, under the watchful eyes of his associates, when he'd gone upstairs to his office.

Once upstairs, she came to a long hallway with unmarked doors on either side. She'd never seen which door he went in. Would it be too much to ask for a name placard? Apparently. Only two doors were labeled—Men and Women—at the far end of the hall. Vanessa started with the door farthest from the restrooms and tried the keys each in turn.

None fit.

She made her way methodically down the hallway, trying all the keys in every door, hoping, praying, wondering if perhaps she'd already tried Jeff's door and failed to open it in her haste.

Finally, at the last door before the men's room, she slid a key into the lock and turned the knob. Immediately, she knew she'd come to the right place. There was Jeff's mug sitting *next* to a coaster. She'd thought his coaster aversion was something he did only at home, just to irritate her, but apparently his disdain for them ran deeper than that. She even caught a whiff of his familiar cologne.

Oh, dear Lord, help me now. If there's evidence here, help me find it.

She turned on the computer and, while it was powering up, fit the small keys into the filing cabinet and desk drawers.

The papers in the filing cabinet were arranged in neat files. She found page after page of numbers on grids, years, incoming, expenses—but no words pointing to the true sources of the funds. While most of the crime ring's income came from human trafficking and drugs, nonetheless, Vanessa was aware of at least one of their cover operations—selling luxury goods for vastly inflated prices. Few people actually bought their ten-thousand-dollar handbags or five-hundred-dollar key chains, but all the documents in the filing cabinet seemed to indicate their money came from those sources.

Disgusted, Vanessa slid the last drawer closed and turned her attention to the computer. She'd always enjoyed using computers before Jeff took her. He, of course, wouldn't let her online at all, not until after Abby was born. Then, out of his reluctance to let her take the baby to any more medical appointments than was absolutely necessary, he'd let her research any of Abby's sniffles and rashes online—as long as he was in the same room to be sure she didn't visit any social networks or do anything to reach out for help.

After every time Jeff let her use the internet, he always checked her browser history afterward, so Vanessa knew well how to check the sites he'd visited recently. Reading through his browser history, she skimmed past the familiar website names, instead checking those that sounded suspicious.

On the third try, she got a sign-in page.

Members Only.

The login name was already entered. The password box held ten black dots.

Enter.

The page that appeared made her stomach turn. Human trafficking, in all its sordid wretchedness.

So visceral was her response, it took her a moment to

realize the vibration she felt was coming from her pocket and not her racing heart.

Debbi's phone. She pulled it out and glanced at the screen. Two men.

That was all. Obviously Eric had been in too much of a hurry to type any more information. She must not have much time.

She glanced around the room. There was nowhere to hide. The computer—she didn't dare leave it turned on. What if whoever had arrived came into this room? It seemed likely enough they would—anyone visiting the office at this hour might well be there because of Jeff's death.

Vanessa shut down the computer, then opened the door just a crack. She peeked into the hallway but saw no one, heard no signs of life. Quickly, she darted out, hoping to reach the stairs, but at that moment, a dull boom sounded, and voices fluttered up from the foyer.

The boom was the main door opening. They were coming in the front door. She couldn't go down the stairs, not with them coming in that way. She glanced behind her, hoping to see an exit sign, but there was nothing but the row of locked doors behind her.

She was trapped, with no escape.

"His office is upstairs." Virgil's voice echoed through the open stairway from below. The man who'd killed Jeff was on his way, and he wasn't alone.

FIVE

Eric sent the text the instant the headlights swept across the parking lot.

He recognized the vehicle. It was the same Land Rover from the news broadcast, the same SUV Virgil had stood in front of in Jeff Nelson's driveway as he'd thrown all of the greater Chicago area into a manhunt for an innocent woman.

Silently, Eric crept from his car, crouching behind the Dumpster, phone in hand. The men who exited the vehicle were arguing in what he supposed were intended to be hushed tones—he couldn't make out any clear phrases—but their anger caused their voices to carry in heated bursts.

Somebody was furious, and they were headed inside.

Oh, dear Lord, keep Vanessa safe. He almost wished he'd gone in with her—except that then she'd have no warning that the men were on their way inside. No, it was better this way. And maybe he could even get a picture of them. The more evidence they had, the better.

As the men passed under the bright beam of the security light, Eric pointed his phone's camera in their direction. The phone's description had touted its picture-taking capabilities—Eric had bought it to catch action shots of the high-school basketball team he coached. He'd never tested its prowess in taking pictures in low light.

He pressed the button and prayed—not just for a clear picture, but for Vanessa, who was still in the building.

The men went inside, and the door slammed closed behind them with a boom.

Vanessa darted into the ladies' room, settling the door closed silently as angry voices echoed up the stairs. She glanced around the room, grateful to see two stall partitions instead of an open room. Deftly, she stepped into a stall, pulled the door closed behind her and stood on the seat so her feet wouldn't be seen. It didn't seem likely the men in the hall would enter the women's restroom, but she was going to take every precaution she could. If they even so much as realized Jeff's computer was still warm or suspected something might be out of place—she'd resisted the temptation to place his mug on the coaster—it wouldn't take them long to look in the ladies' room, not with all the other doors locked.

The voices echoed louder as the men proceeded down the hall in her direction. She tensed, waiting, while keys jingled in the hallway, and then the echoes shifted. The voices continued, the words no longer muted by the heavy bathroom door, but tinny, crisp, almost amplified.

She jolted and nearly slipped from her perch on the commode before she realized the men were not in the room with her. Their words were funneled through the ductwork to the ventilation opening above her head, Virgil's voice sounding just as it did when it resonated through the vents in her Barrington basement.

"—ran outside the second we heard the crash. She never drove past the house—just out the backyard and straight for the highway. There's no way she's hiding in the neighborhood."

"What about her sister?"

"We've kept surveillance on her since sundown. Dick's guys are going to run a job. No sign of any unusual activity."

Vanessa felt her heart freeze, then slowly start beating again. So, they knew about Alyssa. Jeff had known about Alyssa, so she wasn't too surprised the others knew about her. Fortunately, from the sound of it, they didn't know about Sammy. Alyssa must be keeping him out of sight, just as she'd figured she would. That much was a relief. But how long would Alyssa be able to keep him hidden, now that these men were watching her?

The conversation continued. "What about her other friends from high school? Other family connections? She had to go somewhere." The firm voice sounded like a drill sergeant delivering a lecture.

Virgil's voice had never sounded so wheedling, so pleading. "Maybe she's still driving. If she left the state, kept going out of the range of the television broadcasts—"

"With two little kids and a baby? All by herself? She'd have to stop for gas. Jeff's credit cards haven't been used, have they?"

There was a pause, clicking of keys. Vanessa could picture them using Jeff's automatic log-in to check his accounts. Knowing the guys he worked for, every credit card was accounted for, probably procured through them.

"Nope." Virgil grunted. "She could use cash."

"Maybe." The other man's voice sounded distantly familiar. Vanessa tried to recall where she'd heard it before. It wasn't one of Virgil's usual guns—no, those goons didn't talk back or ask questions. This guy sounded as if he was bossing Virgil around. Could he be the ringleader? With a breach like this one, it made sense the head honcho would swoop in to make sure all the holes were properly plugged. "No. No, she'll be in hiding. She's scared, doesn't know where to go. She'll panic, go somewhere familiar."

"There was that cabin."

"Cabin?"

Vanessa felt her heart nearly stop at the word. They knew about the cabin? Surely it wasn't the same place....

"Her grandpa's cabin. Yeah, we found out about that when her grandpa died. She and her sister were supposed to inherit half each. The sister had her declared legally dead and sold the cabin."

"So the sister sold the cabin—" the bossy voice protested.

"But Madison doesn't know they sold the cabin."

"She doesn't?"

"How would she? Jeff didn't let her know anything."

Slowly, Vanessa's heart started beating again, but with dread-filled thumping. They knew about the cabin. They knew more than she did. It was worse than she'd thought.

"Have you checked the cabin?"

"I don't—" Virgil's wheedling rose to a new, wordless level.

"You don't *what?*" The bossy voice grew angrier.

"I don't know where it is. But I can find it. I can. No problem. I'm on it."

"You bet you're on it. Do we have everything we need here?"

"Everything." The keys rattled and jingled, and the voices shifted to muffled sounds as the men entered the hallway and headed toward the stairs.

Vanessa held her breath, listening carefully. Were they gone? She didn't dare leave the restroom until the men had left the building, but how could she know when they were gone? There wasn't a window in the bathroom.

And she didn't have time to wait. Virgil was going to check the cabin. She had to get her girls out of there, get them long gone before Virgil and his men arrived.

Her enemies were already two steps ahead of her.

Eric climbed back into the car but kept his eyes on the office building. He could see only the main set of doors from where he sat, but that was really all he needed to see. The Land Rover hadn't moved, and Vanessa hadn't appeared. All he could do was pray that Vanessa had received his text in time, that she'd get low and stay low until after the men were gone.

Finally, just as he was beginning to worry that they'd been inside too long and were going to stay until everyone else arrived for the day, the doors opened and the men exited, climbed into the Land Rover and backed out of their parking spot.

Trading quick glances between the door and the SUV, Eric watched the vehicle roll out of the parking spot onto the access road. They'd made it to the stoplight but were still within his line of sight when the doors of the office building opened again and Vanessa peeked out.

She glanced around, then darted for his car, a bulky box that looked like a slimline desktop CPU tucked under her arm.

The stoplight turned green. The Land Rover moved forward, veered wildly wide, then swung around in an abrupt U-turn.

Vanessa was wide out in the open. Either the criminals had spotted her and turned around to come after her, or they'd forgotten something and turned back to get it. Either way, they'd see her soon enough.

He had to get her out of there.

Starting the car, he put it in Reverse and backed up wide, clear of the trees, then pointed the car toward Vanessa, aiming the passenger side at her path, opening the door just as he reached her.

"Get in!"

She dived inside, and he kept moving even as she pulled her legs in. He'd kept his distance from her thus far out of respect for what she'd been through, but safety was more important than feelings. He grabbed her arm, tugging her into the vehicle as she pulled the door shut after her. She dumped the CPU on the floor mat and buckled her seat belt. "Are they gone?"

"Not quite." He'd let go of her arm to steer with both hands as he stomped the gas to stay ahead of the vehicle that pursued them.

Squealing tires added emphasis to his words as the Land Rover took a sharp corner into the parking lot.

Eric's Mustang slid down a grassy median into the next lot. He accelerated toward the access road and the stoplight, which was turning yellow.

Gunning the engine, he made it through just as it turned red above him.

Vanessa looked behind them. "They ran the red light. They're catching up. Do you know where you're going?"

"I have a few ideas, but I'm guessing those guys know the neighborhood better than I do." He got back on the highway and headed out of the city. It was probably a good idea to stay near traffic, thin as it was, for now— with more witnesses around, the criminals might be less likely to try anything.

But Vanessa had more bad news. "They know about the cabin, too."

"Our cabin?"

"Yes. I overheard them talking while I was hiding inside. They've been watching my sister—they said something about guys running a job? I don't know what that means. I hope they leave her and Sammy alone."

"They're too busy chasing us—" Eric's words were cut off by a sharp sound behind them, and he ducked instinctively. "They're shooting at us?"

As if to answer his question, another shot sounded.

Vanessa ducked low.

Eric slid down as far as he could in his seat. He needed to be able to see to drive and didn't dare let the shots scare him into slowing down. Surely that was what the men behind them wanted—they weren't likely to hit much, especially not given his car's low profile. But their boxy Land Rover was another story. It sat high above its own tires, exposing them to a direct hit. Vanessa had been quite the shot back in the days when her grandfather taught her marksmanship.

"Your grandfather's shotgun is in the backseat, along with a box of shells."

Vanessa didn't hesitate, but reached back and grabbed them.

"Do you remember—"

"Grandpa taught me how to shoot with this gun. Of course, it's been a long time." She rolled down her window as she spoke.

"Are you sure you know what you're doing?"

"Keeping these guys from hurting my kids."

Eric felt something swell in his throat. This was the Vanessa he knew, not the cowering accused murderer who'd showed up at his cabin. Inwardly, he cheered that his old friend hadn't lost her spirit, in spite of all she'd been through. But there were far more urgent concerns for him to worry about. "Yeah, I know. But I mean—aim for their tires. Try to shoot them out. That's buckshot. You get four balls—"

"I know how buckshot works." Vanessa twisted her torso around in the seat and angled her head and arms out the window, aiming the gun behind them. She raked her flying hair back from her face and, with speed that surprised him, fired.

"Ouch, that recoil," she muttered, rubbing her shoulder as she slid back into her seat. "Did I hit anything?"

Eric studied the rearview mirror. "Not that I can tell, not yet. But I think you made them nervous. They stopped shooting and backed off a little."

While Vanessa loaded the next slug, Eric realized there

was something more urgent they needed to be doing. "I think we need to call the county sheriff's office. Tell them to go to the cabin, warn Debbi, tell her to get the girls out of the cabin. If these guys send a team or if they shoot out one of our tires, we might not get a chance to warn her—"

He fell silent as Vanessa met his eyes, saw the battle she waged to make the decision. For Vanessa, calling the authorities was a risk that meant she might end up behind bars herself....

Vanessa made a strangled sound as she pulled out Debbi's phone. "I don't have a choice. These guys know about the cabin, the sales transaction—they'll know about you shortly, if they don't already. It's the only way to keep the girls safe. If that means I get arrested for murder, well, at least my daughters will be safe."

"Okay, but don't dial 911 here, or you'll get the Chicago authorities, and they're all looking to arrest you. Call the nonemergency number of the county sheriff's office." Eric knew the number, having had to call it several times in the past year when a rash of vandals disturbed his property and that of his neighbors. As he recited the numbers, Vanessa dialed.

"Yes, this is Vanessa Jackson. I'd like to report—" Her voice caught, and she placed her hand over her mouth for a moment. "Yes, *that* Vanessa Jackson. I was kidnapped by a man who went by the name of Jeff Nelson." Another pause. "Yes, that Jeff Nelson. Listen, please—this is important. My daughters are at a cabin with a friend of mine, but the men who killed Jeff are on their way there."

Another pause, then Vanessa continued, her patience straining in her voice as shots continued to echo behind them. "Yes, these men killed Jeff, and now they're headed to the cabin. Please, get my girls out safely, but don't scare them." Her voice cracked, but she steadied it quickly. "We have a trust password. Use it, and they'll know I want them to go with you. It's *Jabberwocky*."

His attention focused on the road, his speed and staying ahead of their pursuers, Eric was nonetheless surprised by the sudden swelling of emotion he felt at the name of the old poem that had been so special to them growing up. Vanessa may have been gone for eight years, but she hadn't ever forgotten, had she? No, she'd treasured the same memories he'd looked back upon with such fondness.

Vanessa rattled off the cabin's address. Then, after some thanks and more urgings to do their best not to frighten the girls or Debbi, Vanessa ended the call, stowed the phone and cleared her throat, erasing some, but not all, of the pain from her voice.

"I had to shoot high to avoid hitting your rear spoiler." Vanessa turned her attention quickly to the men shooting at them from behind, and was now scooting into the window, shotgun in hand. "Do you think you can swerve right a tick when I say *now?*"

Eric quickly assessed the terrain, impressed at how quickly she'd swallowed her emotions and switched her focus to deal with the issue at hand. But then, she'd probably learned that skill in captivity—trying to balance the demands of her captor with the needs of her children. It was a learning experience he wouldn't wish on anyone, but it had given her a skill set that rose to the challenge before them now.

"Eric?" Vanessa prompted, the gun ready in her hands.

Time for him to focus on the moment, to rise to the challenge before them. The road was four lanes wide, and traffic was thin at this hour of night. "No problem."

"Now."

He swerved.

She shot.

SIX

Framed by his rearview mirror, the Land Rover behind them behaved as though it had hit something, swerving wildly and stuttering to a stop. "You took out their tire!" Eric announced as Vanessa slid back into her seat. Joy and relief surged through him, as well as admiration for his old friend. The Vanessa he'd known long ago could have easily made that shot, but to make it after eight years of being locked away... She was a survivor, wasn't she? He'd long ago had a crush on her, but now something more was added to that, a more mature kind of love. He admired her and was proud of her.

"Thank God." She sighed with relief and buckled her seat belt again.

"Yes, thank God," Eric echoed, curious now how much she meant the words. Vanessa had been through a horrible ordeal. Had she retained her faith? His had been shaken by her disappearance, though he'd realized after an angry couple of years that if Vanessa was still alive, he needed God to watch over her, and he'd started going to church every week to pray for her.

But for right now, they had so many more pressing things to discuss. With the Land Rover fading quickly from sight, Eric turned his attention to the question that had been burning inside him since the moment Vanessa peeked her head out the office-building door. "You found evidence?"

"On Jeff's browser history. I brought the computer, plus these pages from his file cabinet." She held up a sheaf of papers he hadn't noticed before. "They're ledgers with source codes. The numbers are big. They demonstrate that a lot of money was involved. Between the two of them, we've got enough to show there was a huge crime ring, even identify some of the conspirators. Now, whether we can figure out who was behind it, I don't know. I think that guy who was with Jeff is his boss, but I don't know who he is. His voice sounded vaguely familiar. I just can't place it."

"I tried to take pictures of them as they went inside." Eric wished he had something more helpful to tell her. "But it was dark out, and with no flash, who knows if we'll get anything. They were standing under that security light—"

"It was a very bright security light." Vanessa sounded wistfully hopeful, but her optimism was distinctly guarded. "Thank you for taking the pictures. Can I see?"

Eric handed her the phone and she scrolled through the pictures. "They're so blurry. It's hard to see in the dark. Maybe with a full-size screen, indoors—"

"We can upload them to a computer. I have the download cable in my glove box."

"Where do we want to do that?" Vanessa made a hiccuping sound.

Eric feared she was already regretting the phone call she'd placed, which might have serious repercussions. Hopefully, her children were safe. For now. But would the authorities allow her to see them again, or would they believe she was a murderer and lock her away? "I'm sorry that we had to call the sheriff's office."

Vanessa sniffled, and Eric glanced at her, afraid she was going to break into tears.

But she composed herself. "It's for the best. I couldn't keep them safe, alone." Her voice broke.

"You did an amazing job."

"If you hadn't been there—" Vanessa shook her head, as though denying his claim "—I'd be asleep at the cabin with my girls right now, with those men on their way. I'd have no idea."

Eric reached over and took her hand, felt a connection he'd only dared to hope he might feel. She gave his palm a slight squeeze. Did she feel it, too? He hoped so. Prayed so. Because now that she was back in his life, he didn't want to let go. "It's okay. I was there. The authorities are going to get Debbi and the girls out. Everything is going to be okay."

"Is it?"

Much as he wished he could offer her some proof, Eric didn't honestly know. How fast would Virgil's men arrive at the cabin? They had to change a flat tire, but how long would that take? Would the sheriff's deputies get to Debbi and the girls in time? And then, would the authorities believe her story? Would Vanessa's evidence be enough? And—most important—would they be able to figure out who was really behind the crime ring? If they couldn't cut off the head, chopping off an arm would only anger the monster. He didn't know a great deal about criminals, but could guess that much for certain.

Vanessa cleared her throat. "I'm so sorry for dragging you and Debbi into this."

"We're glad to help."

"You can't be." She made a sound that was almost laughter, though it was weighed down by heavy emotion.

"I am," he insisted, squeezing the hand he still held. "When you disappeared, I vowed to do anything and everything. I knocked on doors, hung up posters. Raged at the world. Remember that old gnarled tree in the woods?"

"Our monster?"

"I chopped it down with an ax."

"You left it dead?" She quoted the poem again. This time her attempt at laughter sounded a little lighter, tinged by hope.

"I wanted to slay the monster that took you. I prayed God would give me the chance. One chance to storm the castle and bring you back, if only He'd show me where you were." Eric cleared his throat, realizing how dramatic his words probably sounded, even if they were all completely true. "And now you're here. And I'm glad. I'm glad to help."

Vanessa said nothing, but pulled her hand free of his. Eric glanced away from the road just long enough to see her wipe away tears.

"Vanessa?"

"I'm okay. It's okay." She composed herself. "I just wish I'd known…before I went with Jeff."

Her voice faded to almost nothing, but Eric still heard her. He heard, too, what she'd left unspoken. She'd gone with the kidnapper because Jeff had treated her as if she was someone special, as if she was beautiful. Maybe if Eric had figured out how to tell Vanessa how he'd felt about her before she met Jeff, the kidnapper wouldn't have found such an easy target.

Eric had failed her. Worse than that, looking back now, he distinctly remembered things he'd said, negative comments he'd made to her in an effort to disguise how he really felt. Even the day he'd dressed up as the highwayman, he'd treated it like a joke rather than confess his feelings. Who was he to think he could defeat that monster? He'd practically shoved her into Jeff's arms.

If she hadn't needed his help tonight, she probably wouldn't even speak to him. He wouldn't blame her.

"Where do you want to go next? To the county sheriff's office, to see your girls?"

Vanessa let out a thoughtful breath. "I don't think I'm ready to go to the sheriff's office, not yet, not until I know the evidence I've gathered is enough to defend my innocence. If I walk in there unprepared, I might not get the chance to walk out."

"So, where do you want to go? We'll need to upload the pictures from my phone, plug in the computer... Do you want to go to my house?"

"The cabin is a lot closer. I need to make sure my girls got out okay."

"But Virgil—"

"We're ahead of him. We know we're ahead of him now. Besides, when Virgil's boss asked him about the cabin, he said he hadn't checked it yet because he didn't know where it is."

"He can get the address from public record, probably find it online. GPS will do the rest. It won't take long."

"And they have to change a flat tire. We have time to look at the evidence I've gathered, to decide if we have enough to prove my innocence."

"And if we don't?"

"I'll make that decision once I see what we've got."

"At the cabin," Eric concluded, pressing his foot a little harder on the accelerator. "We can go there, make sure the girls got out okay, view the pictures. I know the fastest way to get there that saves a good ten minutes off the fastest route any GPS will recommend. I don't know how long it's going to take them to change that tire, but I don't want to find out."

For the next few minutes, he tried to focus on driving, on getting to the cabin as quickly as possible. But focusing on anything other than the woman beside him was extremely difficult. He still didn't see how they were going to get through the night—evading both the human-trafficking ring and the police.

Then a ringing sound cut through the silence. The phone Vanessa had used earlier to call the police lit up with an incoming call. Vanessa looked at the screen and swallowed hard. "It's the county sheriff's office—they're calling me back."

"I guess you should answer it."

"I guess so." Vanessa's voice trembled, but she answered the ringing phone.

Eric wished he could hear the other side of the conversation, but he was able to gather quite a bit by what Vanessa said.

"They weren't too scared? Good. Thank you, I appreciate that." Her voice hitched, and when Eric glanced her way, he saw strain on her face. "Yes. What Debbi has told you is all true. I have evidence. A computer and some files. We were headed for the cabin." She paused, and her voice became quieter, more reluctant. "We'll meet you there." She closed the call.

"The sheriff's office is sending someone to meet us at the cabin?" Eric guessed.

"Yes. Two deputies. They want to have a look at the evidence we gathered."

Eric felt a mixture of anxiety and relief. He knew Vanessa was risking a lot by meeting with the deputies, but he couldn't help feeling slightly safer knowing armed officers of the law would be there, when and if Virgil and his men showed up. The trick, of course, would be convincing the police that Vanessa wasn't a murderer—and getting them on their side before the real murderers arrived.

Taking back roads and driving quickly, Eric arrived at the cabin to discover a county sheriff's vehicle parked outside.

Vanessa grabbed the evidence she'd gathered and gave

him a quick, frightened look. But then, with not a moment to waste, she hopped from the vehicle and hurried toward the cabin, clutching the CPU to her chest.

Knowing they wouldn't have much time before Virgil and the other thugs showed up, Vanessa forced herself to run toward the cabin's front door, instead of away from it. Somehow, knowing the deputies were probably waiting on the other side was even more terrifying than facing the shotgun Eric had held—probably because she knew Eric and trusted him deep down, on a level she hadn't trusted anyone in a long time. And Jeff had made terrible claims about what would happen if she ever tried to go to the authorities—of how he'd counter her story, offer lies and fabricated evidence as proof, how he'd get custody of their children and leave her to rot in jail.

But Jeff was dead now.

She burst in the front door to find two uniformed officers waiting for her. A woman who appeared to be in her mid-forties stood by the kitchen counter, and a younger man stood from the couch as she stepped inside.

"I'm Vanessa Jackson," she announced. The sweet relief of using her own name after so many years helped to ease her fear.

The younger officer approached her. His name badge said Perez. He asked Vanessa, "Do you have any identification?"

"No. Everything was taken from me." She realized as she spoke the words how true they were. Jeff had taken everything—her innocence, her identity, her instinct to trust others. Even now, she wondered if the deputies would believe her and try to help her or keep her girls from her and lock her away, just as Jeff had threatened.

"The incident earlier this evening in a Chicago suburb..." Officer Perez began.

Vanessa gulped a breath, trying to think how best to begin her defense. Jeff had hated every word she'd ever used to defend herself, had beat her into submission until she only stood up for her kids, never for herself. She'd take any beating if it meant protecting her kids. Now the words froze in her throat, her shoulders tensing instinctively to resist the blows.

She couldn't speak.

Eric stomped on the rug behind her as he entered. He voiced her defense, relaying everything just as she'd told him. "Virgil Greenwood, the man in the news broadcast who claimed he discovered the body—he didn't discover it. He murdered the man. Vanessa drove away to keep the kids safe. She was kidnapped eight years ago by this human-trafficking ring. She has evidence."

To Vanessa's relief, Perez didn't look overly skeptical at the news. Instead his eyebrows went up in a curious, open expression as he reached for the CPU.

"We'd like to see the evidence." He held out his hands, his expression guarded, cautious.

Would he really believe them? Vanessa didn't have time to worry about it. If Virgil and his men were on their way, she had to earn the trust of the police quickly.

As Vanessa handed over the CPU, the officer told her, "I remember when you went missing. I always thought, with you working at a restaurant near the interstate, somebody probably took you and drove away. Debbi, the woman who was here with the girls, filled us in a little on your story."

"And my girls are—"

"They're with child protective services. They're trained in helping kids in difficult times. They're safe."

Vanessa tried to smile, to show her appreciation that he was willing to hear her side of the story and maybe even help, but at the same time, it was so hard hearing that her daughters were in protective custody. Would she get them back? Only if she could prove her innocence.

But first, the deputy had another question. "According to the news report, you also have a son. Where is he?"

"I left him with my twin sister, Alyssa."

The officer nodded, looking down at the CPU in his hands as though trying to decide what to do with it.

Eric stepped past him. "We can hook that up to my laptop. Just let me grab it." He bounded up the stairs two at a time.

"We need to hurry," Vanessa explained. "The men who killed Jeff are on their way here—that's why I needed to get the girls to safety."

"How do you know they're coming here?"

While Eric connected the CPU to the laptop, Vanessa explained briefly about what she'd overheard, including her suspicions about the real head of the monster. "Virgil Greenwood may have pulled the trigger, but he's not the head of the crime ring."

"Do you know who is?" The female deputy had been hovering, listening to Vanessa's story.

"It's a man." Vanessa explained what she knew. "I've heard his voice. I recognize it but can't quite place it."

Eric finished connecting the computers and now held out his phone and the download cable. "I saw the man and took a couple of pictures, but it was dark out. I don't know what we'll get."

"Let's see them."

Eric connected the phone to the laptop.

Vanessa watched him work, her heart swelling with gratitude for all Eric had done to help her—especially his willingness to take her side and explain things when words failed her. After everything Jeff had put her through, her heart warred against the thought of trusting anyone, especially a man. But Eric was so completely different from Jeff.

Years before, she'd wished Eric cared for her the way she cared for him. But maybe he had. Maybe he still did. At the thought, her heart yearned with a depth of longing that surprised her. Did she want Eric to care for her? On the one hand, all she'd been through with Jeff made her wary. But Eric was so very different from Jeff. Helpful instead of hurtful. Tender instead of terrifying. He was everything she'd longed for all these years, everything Jeff wasn't.

There wasn't time to dwell on the difference. The pictures started uploading from the camera on Eric's phone. One blurry image filled the screen, then another, the outlined figures of men smeared across the front of the building.

"It was too dark." Deputy Perez shook his head regretfully. "With no flash, it increases the exposure time. You have to hold perfectly still—"

But as he spoke, a clearer image filled the screen—this one with one face pointed directly at the camera, unobstructed by the other man.

Vanessa sucked in a sharp breath. "Arthur Sherman."

"Arthur Sherman," Eric repeated. "Isn't he the guy who owns the Flaming Pheasant restaurant chain?"

Perez turned to Vanessa. "Does he fit the voice you recognized?"

"Yes." Vanessa pinched her eyes shut against the flood of memories. "That's why I recognized his voice—oh, my!"

"What?" Eric sounded concerned and took a step closer to her.

Vanessa reached for him, to lean on him for support, surprised when his hand held her, steady yet firm, supportive without hurting. It wasn't a feeling she was at all accustomed to, but it was one she desperately needed right now. And he kept her upright. "He interviewed me before I was hired. He asked me questions about my family, about not having parents, just a grandfather. He made it sound like he wanted to make sure I'd have alternate means of transportation if I had trouble getting to work, but that wasn't it at all, was it?"

Deputy Perez looked angry. "There are Flaming Pheasant restaurants up and down the interstate highway system, across several states. Not too many in any one state, so they're spread out over jurisdictions. If girls went missing here and there, especially if they didn't have parents or close family to file a report when they went missing—"

Eric looked equally disgusted. "He could target vulnerable girls all over the country, have his boys whisk them away one night, and there might not even be a missing person's report for the authorities to use to see a pattern."

"Their employer certainly wouldn't file one," Vanessa concurred, seeing the picture all too clearly now, leaning heavily on Eric as the reality weighed upon her, threatening to pull her to the floor. "I always wondered how the restaurant chain could be so popular when we never had too many customers. The food isn't very good."

"But if his main source of income isn't the restaurant or the food—" Perez shook his head "—he can afford to keep the restaurants open as a cover for his real business. I'm going to call the station, have them run a search on missing-person reports all over the country and see how many have ties to the Flaming Pheasant. I think we're onto something."

"But what about the evidence on the CPU?" Vanessa asked.

Even before she had the question asked, Perez stepped off to the side, speaking into the microphone of the radio-communications set he wore.

The female officer, whose name badge identified her as Deputy Abbott, explained, "If this is half as big as I think it is, the FBI is going to want that information. Our office doesn't have the manpower to field an investigation of this magnitude. We need to call in the big guns—but before we place that call, we need to see if my partner's theory is correct. This shouldn't take long."

While Perez spoke to the authorities running the search at the station, Vanessa turned to face Eric, still leaning on him, needing his strength, but still unsure where she stood with him after so many years. She could see the disgust on his face that had been triggered by the realization of what Arthur Sherman was up to—but she couldn't help wondering how much of that disgust extended to her, for getting caught up in such sordid crimes.

SEVEN

Anger and revulsion warred inside him. Eric tugged Vanessa securely against him, wishing he could have shielded her from harm as easily as he held her now. For how many years had Arthur Sherman been using his restaurant chain as a cover operation so he could traffic girls? Too many. They had to put a stop to him—soon, before he had a chance to destroy evidence or, worse yet, go into hiding. Then they might never catch him. He could continue to get away with his crimes, and his other victims might never be liberated.

As long as Arthur Sherman remained at large, Vanessa wouldn't be safe. The man who'd stolen so much from her could still silence her testimony—even that of her children. None of them would truly be free until he was brought to justice.

In the meantime, they still had every reason to believe Virgil and Arthur were headed to the cabin. He wasn't sure how long it would take them to arrive, but they might not have much time. "We've got to do something," he whispered to Vanessa.

Vanessa looked up at him, so close he could see the moisture that welled in her eyes, the fear and the emotion she had to fight back in order to press on in her fight for freedom. "Deputy Perez is waiting to hear—"

Eric wanted to fight with her, to fight for her. They needed to act. "Yes, but how long is that going to take? Arthur Sherman was in the Land Rover with Virgil. They know you took the CPU from Jeff's office—they had to have seen you carrying it as you ran across the parking lot, and even if they didn't, a simple check of the office will tell them it's gone. They know about the cabin. They know you have evidence against them. They're bound to do one of two things—either go into hiding or come after you."

"They could do both," Vanessa concluded frankly. "Even if Sherman leaves the country, he can issue a hit from a distance. I may have been kept on the periphery, but Jeff always made the threats clear. I know enough of his operations to know that he can reach me even if I can't reach him."

Eric realized she'd been subjected to worst-case scenarios for the past eight years. And she was probably right in her guess, too.

"That's why we've got to do something. Now. Tonight. Before they have a chance to hide or to hurt you."

Vanessa pinched her eyes shut and blew out a long breath. Eric could tell she was thinking. He adjusted his arms around her, and she leaned closer, resting her forehead against his shoulder. Tender feelings flooded his chest. He had to keep this woman safe. But how?

"We're not going to find him," she murmured, eyes still closed. "As long as he even thinks there's a chance I could ID him, he's going to keep his head down. He's smart. He wouldn't have kept this ring going for so many years if he wasn't smart." As she mulled over her theory aloud, she pulled back from his shoulder, looking into his face as though to see if he agreed with her thoughts.

Eric watched her as she spoke, enthralled by the unexpected joy of seeing her again, of watching her lips move as she pieced together her thoughts. Maybe the years hadn't

been the best for her, but she still looked good. A little pale
and perhaps underfed. Her dyed-blond hair was a little dis-
orienting. But she was Vanessa. Not the teen he'd cared for
so long ago, but still, somehow, the same person.

Her next words pulled his attention from her face to
her message.

"There's no way around it. We're going to have to draw
him out."

"Arthur?" Eric asked, so taken aback he almost thought
he'd misheard. "How?"

"You already said he might come after me."

"I don't *want* him to come after you."

"But we need to catch him. If we don't, he could catch
up to me and the kids anytime, days, months, even years
from now. We'll never be safe. My kids won't ever be
safe." She spoke with determination flashing in her eyes
in spite of the tired rings that circled them. Unlike Eric,
who'd at least slept before Debbi had awakened him, Vanessa hadn't slept at all.

Eric was tempted to reach for her hand again, but recalled the way she'd pulled her hand from his before.
"What are you suggesting?"

"He wants the evidence against him, right? He wants
the CPU and my silence?"

"Yes." Eric felt sweat beading cold on the back of his
neck. What was Vanessa thinking? He knew she was
desperate to protect her kids—the fact that she'd driven
through the back wall of a garage told him that. And he
knew it would take something drastic to pull Arthur Sherman out into the open. That was what worried him.

"He already doesn't trust Virgil—he was upset that
Virgil hadn't checked out the cabin already."

Her words sent Eric's pulse racing. He'd known her
too well long ago not to see what she was getting at, and
he didn't like it.

She turned to address Deputy Abbott, who'd been listening to their conversation while they waited for Deputy Perez's report. Vanessa continued, "He'll want to make sure he gets the evidence, the CPU, my vow of silence. Unless he's changed his plans, he's on his way to the cabin right now, in person, tonight. He'll show up if it means making sure the job is done right. I've heard his voice in my ductwork before. He won't risk a breach."

Eric wasn't sure what she was getting at, but he got a terrible feeling she was proposing a risk he didn't want her to take. "Vanessa, I don't—"

"We need to hide the patrol car. And can we get more officers out here and hide them?" she asked Deputy Abbott.

"What are you proposing?" Deputy Abbott looked far more open to Vanessa's idea than Eric felt.

"If Arthur Sherman shows up here, we need to be ready for him."

Eric placed a hand on her shoulder. "*We?* I think you mean *they.* The sheriff's deputies, the FBI. Not us. He could be here any moment."

"And then what? We hide from him? We're here already. This is our chance. You said yourself we've got to do something. It could be hours before the FBI shows up, if they even agree to come. Arthur could be on a plane to Tahiti by then, or wherever criminals hide out. Who knows? He'll be gone to somewhere we can't reach him, but he could still put a hit out on me. This may be our only chance to catch him."

"Not our chance," Eric corrected her again. "The FBI's chance."

Deputy Abbott had nodded along with everything Vanessa said. "I'll hide the patrol car right now, in case they get here early. Then we'll find out what Perez has learned." She grabbed her keys and headed outside.

Eric took advantage of the relative privacy to grill Vanessa on what she was thinking. "You're going to let the police handle this, aren't you? We don't have to be here. Arthur shows up, the officers jump out and nab him. You don't have to be here."

"I don't want to be here, but—"

"But nothing. Your girls need you." He pulled out his keys. "We can leave now, go find your girls, wait in safety."

"Okay," Vanessa agreed, but qualified, "just as soon as the backup officers get here, we can go."

"What do you mean?"

"I mean Perez and Abbott are two people. How many are in Arthur's car? At least two. They need us."

"They don't need you. Your kids need you."

"This may be our only chance to catch Arthur. He could be here any moment. All I'm saying is, we wait until more officers arrive before we leave."

"No." Eric tugged her back into his arms. She leaned against him without resisting. "We leave it to the professionals."

"There are only two of them. If Arthur gets away…" Vanessa's voice faltered slightly.

Eric pulled back just far enough to see her face. "He wants to kill you."

The fear that glistened in Vanessa's eyes told him she'd already considered that. "How else are we going to catch him? And if we don't, he'll always be out there, wanting to kill me." She sucked in a breath and looked up at him. "I tried, Eric. Don't you think I tried? I tried to run away three different times. Each time, I thought I covered my bases, thought I'd found a way out. I tasted freedom, but this monster has too many arms. He pulled me back each time, found me long before I ever made it home. We've got to cut off the head, Eric. And we've got to do it now, as soon as possible. I am not getting caught again."

Eric felt her desperation. He wanted to slay the monster

for her. He really and honestly did. But he couldn't bear the thought of her facing her enemies again, even if it was only to defeat them. He studied her face, wishing he knew what to say to make her see reason, to make her understand why she couldn't face Arthur in person. Finally, he admitted, "I don't want you to be here."

"Why not?"

The question forced him to analyze how he truly felt. Sure, Vanessa was probably right—they needed to catch Arthur before he went into hiding. They needed to act quickly, and to be honest, he probably wouldn't show his face for anything less than a meeting with her.

That wasn't why Eric didn't want her to stay. His hands fisted at his sides as Vanessa hugged herself. He wanted to hold her, to comfort her, but he hadn't been there for her when she'd needed him eight years ago, so why would she want him near her now?

"Why can't we be here?" she asked again, sounding a little impatient this time.

"Because I already lost you once. I vowed to God, if He brought you back, I'd make things right. I'd keep you safe. I can't lose you again."

Vanessa's heart, already flighty with fear and lack of sleep, gave an odd heave, a kind of gasping sensation almost like a sob. She sucked in a breath.

Eric had looked so angry as they discussed Arthur's involvement and how to catch him. Anger, she could handle. Jeff had been angry all the time. But this confession, this caring?

She wasn't used to those things. Much as she wanted to deny the depth of his feelings, she also wanted them to be true. For so many years, she'd figured she'd never see him again. But now here he was, holding her in his arms as though she belonged there. Did he really care about her, as he said? She wanted him to. She certainly cared about him, so maybe it was possible.

Vanessa was pulled from her thoughts when her stomach growled audibly. She glanced toward Deputy Perez, who stood by the window, deep in conversation with the officers at the station.

As her stomach grumbled again, Vanessa clutched at her midsection, glad for an excuse not to acknowledge Eric's words or the feelings they awakened.

To her relief, Eric seemed equally willing to drop the discussion. For all they knew, Arthur and his men might not arrive for a long time, if at all. But the longer she stalled Eric, the longer she'd be there in case they did show up— even if she wasn't sure what she was going to do then. "You must be hungry," Eric said. "Come on, there's food in the fridge."

"Sure." She followed him to the small kitchenette, where Eric produced a loaf of bread and some cold cuts, pickles and mayonnaise—clearly the sandwich ingredients he'd brought with him for a weekend at the lake. He asked her what she wanted on her sandwich and quickly assembled the meal, including a small bag of chips.

Vanessa felt a little guilty eating Eric's food, but she thanked him, realizing he'd done far more than share his lunch, putting his life on the line as they'd outrun the shooting criminals.

"How about some caffeine to go with that?" Eric asked, pulling a couple of sodas from the fridge.

"It's that or fall asleep standing up," Vanessa acknowledged. Sammy had only recently begun sleeping through the night, but she still wasn't used to being awake for so long at a stretch. And if she was going to be of any help in catching Arthur, she wouldn't likely have a chance to rest anytime soon.

As she gulped down a cool Mountain Dew, Deputy

Abbott came back inside. She and Perez joined them in the kitchen.

Perez filled them in on what he'd learned. "Just as I suspected, four different missing-person females in three different states have ties to the Flaming Pheasant restaurant chain. I put in a call to the FBI and explained everything. They're sending out a team."

Vanessa felt almost nauseated, possibly from the sudden rush of sugar, but more than likely from the officer's announcement. "What about me? Did you tell them—"

"I explained everything. They're glad to hear you've been found and are excited about the possibility that the evidence you've retained might help liberate other missing persons."

Vanessa hung her head, and tears welled up—tears of relief and hope that other girls who'd been taken might also see freedom.

But they'd have to catch Arthur Sherman before any of that freedom would mean a thing.

She already knew Eric wasn't going to back her up on this one—he'd been quite clear that he didn't want her to stay—so she stated her case as clearly as she could. "Arthur Sherman has to realize by now that we're onto him, or soon will be. He's not going to wait around to get caught. And assuming he's sticking to the plan, he could be here any moment."

The deputy studied her face as she spoke. "But we're not ready for him. The FBI guys won't arrive for another half hour at the earliest."

Since Perez had been on the phone while Vanessa had discussed the issue with Eric and Abbott moments before, she now filled him in on what he'd missed—hoping he'd be more open to her plan than Eric had been. "Then we'll have to stall him or catch him ourselves, if we can't stall him."

"How are we going to stall him?"

Vanessa couldn't continue staring down the officer. She studied her soda instead. "He wants to get rid of me and whatever evidence I have. I can set a time to meet with him, after the feds arrive—"

"What's in it for you?" Deputy Perez asked.

Confused, Vanessa explained what she thought was perfectly clear. "Until we capture him, my kids and I won't be safe."

"Yes, I know that," Perez stated. "But if that's all you have, then he'll know it, too. He'll know it's a trap. You have to have a reason—a reason he'll understand, no catch, no strings attached—for why you want to meet with him. Or he won't show his face."

Vanessa pinched her eyes shut. Even in her exhaustion, the officer's words made sense. But what could they do, then?

Eric cleared his throat behind her, and she braced herself for what he was about to say, probably reminding her that it was a foolish idea in the first place.

"This guy killed Jeff, right? Or had him killed? So it stands to reason that Vanessa knows they're coming after her and the kids. Why can't she call him up and tell him she'll turn in all the evidence if he'll leave her alone? She's trading safety for evidence."

Vanessa's heart nearly burst with hope at Eric's words. "Yes—that makes sense, doesn't it? If I gave him all the evidence I have against him, I wouldn't be a threat to him anymore. I call him with the understanding that I want to exchange evidence for my safety—and then we either stall him or catch him ourselves."

"You could offer him the CPU," Perez admitted, "but you have no way of turning over your personal testimony."

"But if I gave him my word—he's got to know I'd do anything to protect my kids, that I'm desperate." Vanessa watched the officer weigh her words and feared he'd decide against her plan. "What other options do we have? If he leaves the country, you'll have no way of getting him back. Don't we have to act fast?"

Perez put his open palms in the air. "The FBI is sending a team. Let me radio them and see what they think."

Vanessa nodded and leaned back against the kitchen countertop, chewing the sandwich that would have tasted delicious under any other circumstances. What else could she do? She hoped Virgil and Arthur didn't show up until after the backup officers arrived, but at the same time, she wasn't going to hide and wait for them to leave if this was the only chance she might have to capture them. If they got away, she and her children would never be safe.

EIGHT

"Mind if I join you?" Eric asked, unsure where he'd go if Vanessa said she wanted to be alone.

"Sure." The lone word was nearly inaudible, but Vanessa's shrug seemed to indicate she was beyond caring about little things at the moment. She wanted to catch Arthur Sherman before he fled the country. Compared to that, his presence next to her didn't mean much.

Eric could understand her frustration. Of course it made sense to try to nab the guy while they still could. She'd never be safe until he was caught—especially not if he had a spoken history of ordering hits against his enemies, regardless of whether he was anywhere around. He could be lounging on a foreign beach when he ordered his men to kill her.

Unless they caught him before he got away.

The only thing that bothered him was her plan to use herself as bait. Everything had happened so quickly, and he knew he needed time to sort out a proper response to Vanessa's sudden reappearance in his life. But one thing he knew for certain: now that she was back, he would never forgive himself if he let anything happen to her again.

Sherman's human-trafficking ring had already stolen the past eight years of her life. Eric couldn't stand the thought that they would take anything more from her.

Much as he didn't want Vanessa to ever put herself in harm's way again, Eric felt a stirring inside him. If Sherman wasn't caught, Vanessa and her children would never know peace. They'd have to live in hiding, always alert for danger...assuming they escaped at all.

It wasn't right. It wasn't fair. It wasn't the kids' fault their father was a criminal. Vanessa loved them dearly, in spite of the horrible circumstances that surrounded their births. As Eric contemplated their situation, he felt his affections swell. Vanessa was right. They had to keep the kids safe, to give them a chance at a normal life.

As a teacher, he'd often been told that he treated his students as if they were his own children. He wasn't sure about that, but Vanessa's kids? He could love them as his own, if he had the chance.

While he was absorbed in his thoughts, Vanessa finished her sandwich and rolled the napkin into a ball. He could hear Deputy Perez, over by the window, speaking intently into his radio. Eric realized this was his best opportunity to talk to Vanessa. He wanted to ask her about her faith.

When she'd disappeared eight years before, he'd had to accept the fact she might be dead. Knowing that she'd been raised in the church, had always taken her faith seriously and loved Jesus, Eric's greatest comfort was his certainty that her soul was safe.

But what had happened to her faith in the past eight years? She'd thanked God in the car earlier, but he needed to know if her words were real or empty. Anything might happen before morning dawned. He had to know his friend would be okay.

"Vanessa?"

"Hmm?" She finished off her can of soda, then met his eyes.

Eric wished he had the luxury of easing into the subject, but he suspected Officer Perez would finish his conversation any moment, and then there would be no more time for him to talk privately with Vanessa. So he had to ask bluntly, "Are you still a Christian?"

Her eyes widened. "I haven't been to church in over eight years. I didn't have the option. Church was one of Jeff's biggest fears. For the same reason, I haven't had a Bible."

"You can be a Christian without those things," Eric reassured her, worried she might think he was judging her.

The fear in her eyes softened. "At first, I was really mad at God that these things happened to me. But after a while, I realized I didn't have anyone else I could lean on, anyone else I could trust. I had to lean on God for strength and support. In some ways, my faith is stronger than ever. God got me and my kids out of that house yesterday. And I like to believe God is going to get me through this, today, one way or another."

"One way or another?" Eric repeated.

"If I have to face Arthur Sherman..." Vanessa's voice wavered, but she fought for control and continued, "I have prayed every day that my kids would escape, that they would never have to live in fear for another minute of their lives. If that means I don't walk away today, I'm okay with that, as long as they're free. That's why I'd rather face these guys and try to capture them than run and live in fear forever. I prayed to God. He brought me this far. I believe God will see me through this."

Eric realized he'd taken her hand again. He opened his mouth to tell her how proud he was of her, how pleased he felt to know her faith was strong and how much he really cared for her.

But Deputy Perez stepped in front of them, clearing his throat before announcing, "The feds will be here in half an hour. They've agreed with your plan to try to call

Arthur Sherman, to lure him here with the promise of a meeting. Once they're in place, you can leave. But there's a very real possibility, if you choose to go through with this, that they might arrive before the feds, and it will be up to us to detain them."

Vanessa didn't hesitate. "They're probably on their way already. At least if I call them it will give us some knowledge of their whereabouts and intentions. We can plan ahead, be ready. We can take them by surprise, instead of the other way around." She stepped away from leaning against the countertop and straightened. "Let's do this."

Vanessa stared at the phone Eric held out to her. "I shouldn't use your phone. That would lead them to you."

"They already know your sister sold me the cabin, right? That's why they're coming here. They trailed my Mustang for miles—I can only assume they know how to look up the plates. You and I are in this together. The only way for me to get out of it is if the FBI catches these guys, same as for you." He pressed the phone into her hands. "If you use a sheriff's deputy's phone, *that* would make these guys suspicious."

Deputy Perez and Deputy Abbott both agreed with Eric's reasoning, so Vanessa took the phone. There was no point in putting off the call any longer. It wouldn't cause the bad guys to arrive any sooner—if anything, she might be able to arrange a meeting time that allowed the feds time to arrive and take positions around the property.

The deputies coached her on what to say. The traffickers had to believe she was calling on her own. The fact that she'd called at all would arouse their suspicions, so she had to present her case from a desperate point of view.

No problem. She felt desperate.

Vanessa's fingers trembled so badly she didn't think she could dial. Fortunately she'd seen Virgil's phone number on Jeff's phone enough times she didn't think she'd ever forget it. The phone rang and rang, until she feared no one would answer.

Finally, just as she was certain her call was going to go to voice mail, Virgil's unmistakable voice answered. "Yeah?"

Slightly thrown off by his unconventional greeting, Vanessa struggled to recall what she'd been planning to say.

"This is Madison Nelson." She gave them the name they knew, and hoped by doing so she might never have to claim the name again. "I want you to leave me alone."

"Now, Madison, you know that's not possible. You've got something that belongs to us. We need it back."

She wondered if they knew what she had. Probably, they'd sent someone to check Jeff's office, and that person had told them what was missing. She wasn't surprised. "If I give it back, will you leave me and my kids alone?"

"I believe we could work something out."

The conversation crawled by, each second ticked off by Vanessa's hammering heart. Virgil and his men were already on their way to the cabin. They were willing to agree to meet her there. They could be there in twenty minutes. Vanessa needed to come alone. If they saw anyone else, or even thought they saw anyone else, the deal would be off.

Her mouth dry, Vanessa could barely ask the important question. "Is Arthur Sherman with you?"

"Who? Why would he be with me?" Virgil's words denied it, but the anger in his voice revealed that he didn't like her knowing the name of his boss.

"He needs to be with you when you come to the cabin," Vanessa insisted.

"We'll see about that. Twenty minutes," Virgil snapped, and the call ended.

Vanessa stared at the phone in her hand, unsure if

the risk she'd taken would even pay off. If Arthur Sherman didn't show, she'd be risking everything for nothing. Granted, they might catch Virgil and his men, but she'd already concluded cutting off an arm would only upset the monster.

Eric stepped forward, took the phone from her trembling hand and wrapped a supportive arm around her. She met his eyes, unsure whether his gaze held apology or hope. The conversation had given them a timeline, but it wasn't the timeline they'd hoped for. The FBI agents had said they'd arrive in half an hour—maybe closer to twenty-five minutes, taking into consideration the time that had passed since Deputy Perez had spoken with them.

And Virgil said he'd be there in twenty minutes—ahead of the agents. And they didn't dare let him see the FBI agents arriving—he'd either run or panic and shoot everyone. Neither option was good.

As long as Virgil didn't arrive early, they'd have twenty minutes to figure out a plan and get everything set up. It wasn't long.

While Perez called the FBI to update them on the result of Vanessa's phone conversation, the other three debated a course of action.

"We'll have to stall them as long as possible," Vanessa reasoned. "The FBI should arrive five minutes after Virgil and his men. Five minutes. We can stall them that long, don't you think?"

"It's going to feel like a long five minutes," Eric reasoned. "Anything could happen in that amount of time. I don't think you should be here. We still have time to get you out, get you to safety."

"And if I'm not here, do you really think they're going to stick around and wait for the feds to show up? Once they get off this road, they can go in any direction. They can disappear and track me down at their leisure. If I don't face them now, with police backup, then I pretty much guarantee I'm going to face them again at the worst possible moment. I know how these guys operate."

"If you really want to face them, you'll need to wear body armor under your clothes," Deputy Abbott told her gravely. "I've got an extra set in the car. Don't think they won't try to shoot you, even after you hand over the evidence."

"I'm fine with that," Vanessa agreed, glad the body armor was available. She'd been facing these guys for the past eight years without nearly so much protection. "I'll do whatever it takes."

Perez coordinated their plans with the FBI agents over the phone. There was no way the agents could get there any sooner, although, based on the information the agents were currently digging up on links to the Flaming Pheasant restaurant chain and missing-person cases, they were willing to dispatch a helicopter. The only catch was, the aircraft would be coming from too far away to arrive any sooner than the vehicles already en route.

That left the four of them, on the ground, to coordinate a plan.

"I'll meet them on the porch, out in the open, where they can see me and you can see me, where the FBI can see them the moment they arrive," Vanessa decided as Abbott laid out her options. "If you guys can lie in wait, ready to intervene if things go south."

"I'll hide in the garage," Perez volunteered, eyeing the property through the window. With the autumn trees and bushes bare of leaves, there were very few hiding places available. "I'll have my gun ready. We want to bring these guys in alive, if at all possible, but I'm not going to risk any harm coming to you. You're our key witness."

"I hid our patrol car in the garage," Abbott informed him. "Take the keys—I'll depend on you to give chase if they try to flee on wheels. I'll take a position in the upstairs window. Assuming they park in front of the cabin, that will give me a vantage point from above. Let me run and fetch that body armor." While the officer hurried outside, Eric turned to Perez.

"Where do you want me?"

Perez frowned. "You're a civilian."

"So?"

"I'm not going to tell you where to go or what to do. In any other situation, I'd tell you to stay far away. But this is your property, and given the circumstances—"

Understanding twinkled in Eric's eyes, and he nodded. "There's a tree stand in the woods, just beyond the cabin. It offers a clear view of the cabin, but it's camouflaged, and they're probably not going to be looking that direction, anyway. I'll take my binoculars and my shotgun—"

Perez clamped a hand on Eric's arm. "You are not an officer of the law. You can use that shotgun for self-defense only."

"If they have a gun, and it's pointed at me—"

"If they have a gun and are using it to threaten you or someone you love—that constitutes self-defense. But bottom line—you shoot somebody, you could be charged with murder. Do you understand?"

Eric's jaw hardened. "I'm not going to break any laws," he promised. "But I'm also not going to sit by and let these guys get away."

"I respect that," Perez assured him, letting go of his arm.

Abbott returned with the body armor. "We are seven minutes to ETA. You need to put this on, and we need to get out of sight." Deputy Abbott looked at Perez. "Boys, a little privacy?"

"One moment." Perez grabbed the CPU and pulled the cover off. "If she really does have to hand this over, just to stall them, I don't want to risk giving away evidence." He glanced around the room. "Got anything heavy I can put in here?"

Eric grabbed a few books off a nearby shelf. "These should weigh the right amount, but if they take a close look at this—"

"FBI should be here by then."

"Should?" Eric repeated.

"We're doing the best we can with very little time to prepare. You have a better idea?"

"I think you two need to hide," Abbott told them both. Then she turned to Vanessa with sympathy. "Are you ready?"

"Ready to end this?" Vanessa reached for the body armor. "You better believe I'm ready."

NINE

The sun was only just starting to rise, spreading a misty haze of illumination across the Illinois hills. In the woods, the autumn leaves had turned brown, but the stubborn oaks wouldn't drop their leaves until the new spring growth pushed out the old. Between the evergreen trees and the brown leaves, Eric would be well hidden. And from his perch on Vanessa's grandfather's old hunting stand, he'd be able to see down the ravine, all the way to the cabin, without anyone spotting him.

He wouldn't be in the way of the FBI agents once they arrived, nor would he tip off the criminals that anyone else was around. He wasn't sure he'd be of any help to Vanessa this far from the cabin, but he also wasn't going to get her in worse trouble by letting on that she wasn't alone. He had his shotgun loaded, ready to defend her in any way he could.

From the vantage point of the tree stand ten feet off the ground, he watched as the professionals set their trap. Abbott took her position inside the cabin on the second floor. He saw her shadow move across the upstairs windows overlooking the porch—the same window through which Debbi had watched Vanessa arrive the night before. She'd have a good view of the yard. If Virgil or any of his men tried to pull a gun, she'd be ready.

When she'd parked the patrol car out of sight, Abbot had pulled Vanessa's scarred Sequoia from the garage and left it sitting in the open, a sign to the traffickers that they'd come to the right place.

Perez hid in the garage.

Vanessa was in the house, alone, except for Abbott upstairs.

Eric hunkered down to wait, praying the traffickers would take their time, maybe even arrive a few minutes late...just not so late that the FBI arrived at the same moment. If that happened, the bad guys would surely flee before they even arrived, and the FBI might never get close enough to chase them down.

Crouched low on the tree stand, Eric made himself as small as possible to avoid detection and kept his eyes trained on the cabin. He couldn't help wishing he could be there beside Vanessa as she waited. He knew she had to be terrified. The deputies had warned her there was still a chance, in spite of her body armor and their protective weapons backing her up, that Virgil and his men could still take her out while she was out in the open. The criminals would be most likely to aim for her torso, head shots being notoriously difficult to make. But even with the bulletproof vest protecting the part of her body they were most likely to hit, she was still vulnerable. Not as vulnerable as she'd be every day of her life, for the rest of her life, if these guys weren't caught...but still vulnerable.

And if Arthur didn't show, none of her sacrifice would even be worth it. They might catch Virgil and his men, but those guys were just one arm of the monster. They had to cut off the head.

Knowing they needed God's help more than anything, Eric prayed Arthur would show and that the bad guys would be caught, every last one of them. And most of all, that Vanessa would be safe.

A small brown bird landed on the tree-stand railing, not a foot away from his face. Eric studied the little animal, reassured that it must not have seen him, to land so close.

It was a sparrow. Recognizing it, Eric was reminded of words from the Bible: *"Don't be afraid; you are worth more than many sparrows."*

Was the bird God's way of reassuring him that everything was going to be okay? Eric tried to recall the context of the verse. Wasn't it something about not fearing those who could kill you? Eric was nearly certain that was how the passage went, having heard it in church mere weeks before, but the verses were so eerily fitting. Was God telling him everything would be okay?

The tiny bird hopped half a turn and faced him; its twinkling eyes blinked and it cocked its head to one side, as if challenging his doubt.

"You are worth more than many sparrows."

Adrenaline and caffeine pulsing through him, Eric was now more awake than he'd been all night. That much was good. His thoughts felt clear for the first time, too, as he prayed for God to wrap His protecting arms around Vanessa.

It was that thought—that image of God holding Vanessa safe in His arms, along with the reassurance of the Bible verse—that got to Eric in a new way. All night, he'd been reacting to the situation as it came to him, first recognizing Vanessa, then realizing she wasn't the murderer Virgil claimed her to be, then helping her, trusting her, endangering himself for her safety.

But now, in the clarity of the morning light, in the midst of prayer, his thoughts weren't reactionary anymore. He cared about Vanessa. He'd always cared about her. It had torn him apart when she'd gone missing. But it was more than that, wasn't it? Her disappearance had cut him so deeply because he'd never had a chance to tell her how he felt about her.

And now, he realized, he still hadn't told her.

For an instant, Eric debated jumping down from the tree stand, running up to the cabin and telling Vanessa how he felt. But a glint of light caught his eye—early-morning sunlight on the windshield of a moving car.

Two cars. The Land Rover, its tire replaced, and a BMW sedan.

They weren't messing around, were they?

Vanessa stepped outside and stood on the porch, the CPU clutched to her chest. It disguised the presence of the bulky body armor she wore under her jacket—the only giveaway that she'd trusted the police enough to go to them, in spite of Virgil's plot to drive her far from any means of help by branding her the murderer.

The morning breeze played with Vanessa's hair, and the sunlight set her cheeks aglow. Eric knew she had to be terrified, but he also knew she'd do anything to keep her kids safe. Affection rose inside him. He had to tell her how he felt, just as soon as this was over.

The vehicles parked at odd angles, the Land Rover mostly in front of the sedan, and Virgil stepped out. Eric couldn't make out his words from this distance, but the man held Vanessa's attention.

Meanwhile, the back door of the sedan opened, out of sight from the cabin. Vanessa couldn't see the man who crept out of the vehicle. Cold fear gripped Eric's heart as he saw a man duck low, crouching just out of Vanessa's sight, a gun clutched in his hand.

TEN

Vanessa focused on taking slow, deliberate steps through the cabin doorway, out onto the small porch. She was trembling so hard, they could probably see her fear from the car. From her years of being around these guys and Jeff, she knew their limits, knew they needed to feel respected and obeyed, or they'd snap.

Given the guns they carried, she didn't want them to snap. But she also didn't want to hand over the CPU until the FBI arrived. It might not take more than a couple of seconds for them to realize the slimline cover held books instead of a hard drive.

Virgil stared her down from his position near the vehicle. He wasn't coming any closer—why not? Were they hoping she'd get so close they could pull her into the car? Or did he suspect she wasn't truly alone? Virgil cleared his throat with a harsh sound. "You're sure you didn't make a copy of any of the information on the computer?"

"How would I even know how to do that? You guys have kept me locked in a basement for the last eight years." Vanessa wanted to scream, but she kept her voice steady, watching Virgil's hands, still far from the gun that seemed to wink at her from under his jacket every time Virgil moved his arms.

They surely had more guns, too. The vehicles had tinted

windows, and the car was almost completely obscured by the SUV. She didn't like it.

Most of all, she didn't like that she couldn't see any sign of Arthur Sherman. If he didn't come, what was the point? If they didn't catch him, she'd never be free, not really.

"What about your friend Eric? This is his cabin."

"He didn't want me to call you. He's not here." The words were all true. Eric had been quite against her calling Virgil, at least in the beginning. And he wasn't technically at the cabin, but in the woods behind it, where she hoped he'd be safe.

"See, that's what concerns me. You don't know where he is, and I don't know that he doesn't have copies of everything on that computer. You're about to hand it over to me—why?" Virgil took one step closer to the porch, then another.

"I want you to leave me and my kids alone." Vanessa couldn't help wondering why, if the criminals figured she'd made copies of the evidence already anyway, they'd bother to show up today. To get the computer back, obviously. And to get what answers they could from her. And then what? She couldn't imagine they'd let her live once they had what they came for.

She raised her eyes just high enough to see past the Land Rover to the road beyond. Still no sign of the FBI. Virgil and his men had arrived precisely when they said they would. If the FBI was on time, they should get there any moment. Were they holding back, biding their time until just the right moment? Or were they running late?

Her heart rammed inside her ribs. Virgil's smile was much too broad, his posture far too confident. They had no intention of letting her live, did they?

Eric watched the gunman creeping along the backside of the BMW sedan and wondered how accurate Vanessa's grandfather's old shotgun would be from that distance. Not nearly accurate enough, and Eric didn't dare take a shot he wasn't sure of making—he'd only tip off the traffickers to his presence and spark a shoot-out. Vanessa was vulnerable either way.

Still, Eric clenched his hands around the gun, taking aim, ready to act should the moment arise. Surely the feds would be arriving soon. He wanted the gunman gone.

His only consolation was that Deputy Abbott in the cabin would be able to see the gunman from her upstairs view. But there was still no sign of any vehicles approaching on the road, and from his perch, Eric could see for a couple of miles or more, before the hills blocked his view. And dust from vehicles approaching on the gravel country roads would be visible farther than that.

The FBI needed to get there soon. They'd said they'd be there. But even if they arrived in the next couple of minutes, would they be able to stop the gunman before he hurt Vanessa?

"Why don't you hand me that computer?" Virgil stood to the side of the steps to the cabin's small porch, little more than an arm's reach away.

"Where is Arthur Sherman? I want to give it to him." Vanessa scanned the vehicles. She could see figures inside, shadowy threats without features or faces. If Sherman didn't show, all her risks would be for nothing. She and her children would have to go into hiding and live in constant fear. Jeff had always claimed no one could hide from them—not even the witness protection program could save her.

And what would happen to Eric? By now, she knew her captors knew about him—that he'd bought the cabin she'd been supposed to inherit, that his Mustang had served as her getaway vehicle, his shotgun had taken out the Land Rover's tires. Virgil had called him by name.

Would Eric be safe if Arthur Sherman wasn't captured? She doubted it. Guilt plagued her. Eric had been so generous to help her. She hated that he'd gotten implicated because of her. But far worse than that, she hated that they hadn't had more time together. If she had to go into hiding, would she even be able to see him? Would she ever get a chance to talk to him about all the things she wanted to discuss?

There were so many things she wanted to ask him, so much she wanted to explore. During her absence, he'd grown into a handsome, capable man. He was brave and strong, and she hated the thought that she'd have to cut short their friendship again, before she had the chance to find out if it was more than just friendship.

It was possible her perspective was a little skewed after everything she'd been through for the past eight years, but she knew her feelings were true. She loved her kids. She hated the criminals who, even now, were trying to outmaneuver her and ruin her life.

And she was pretty sure her feelings for Eric were more than just friendship.

Virgil took his time answering, walking closer, a little to the side of the vehicles. His activity was certainly suspicious, and his words were devastating. "Arthur couldn't make it. You're going to give the computer to me. Now!" The last word was barked like a command, its sudden force almost enough to distract her from what was really happening.

Virgil stood to the side of the steps, out of the way from the rear of the sedan. A man popped up from behind the back of the vehicle, his gun drawn.

Vanessa spun around and dived back toward the open doorway of the cabin while gunfire exploded from the windows above.

* * *

Eric watched in terror as the gunman leaped up, his weapon trained on Vanessa. But at the same instant, shots exploded from the cabin's upstairs windows.

Eric didn't see what happened to the gunman. He was watching Vanessa as she flung herself toward the door, disappearing inside the cabin. Too many shots had sounded. How many rounds had Abbott fired? How many had the gunman gotten off? Eric couldn't tell if any of them had hit Vanessa, and now she was out of sight. Was she okay? She had to be okay. He still had so many things he wanted to tell her—especially how he felt about her. She'd been gone so long, and they'd had such a short time together. He couldn't stand the thought that the gunfire aimed at her might have hit its mark.

The SUV lurched forward while the sedan moved backward, out of the Land Rover's way as it turned wide on the open lawn. The gunman lay slumped, unmoving, even as the car peeled out past him.

Virgil ran toward the SUV, but the garage door flew open and the patrol car pulled out just in time to block the driveway. Neither the Land Rover nor the BMW were going to get out that way.

Eric glanced back toward the cabin, but could see no sign of activity beyond the front door. Was Vanessa okay? Had she been hit?

With the patrol car effectively blocking the driveway, Deputy Perez leaped from the vehicle, gun drawn, while Abbott bounded down from the porch, cuffs ready as she subdued Virgil.

The Land Rover still obscured most of the sedan, at least from the vantage point of the deputies. From the trees, Eric could clearly see the back door of the sedan pop open. A man jumped out and was escaping toward the woods on foot, but the deputies had their hands full, too full to go after him.

At the same moment, clouds of dust rose on the road. The FBI was arriving—but would they be too late? Unfortunately, the crook running toward the woods on foot already had a good head start. Eric could see that much clearly. And he saw something else fairly clearly, too.

The running man was Arthur Sherman. He'd come after all.

But at the rate he was running, he was going to get away. Sherman had found the deer trail that wound down into the ravine. If he followed it for another half mile, he'd reach the road. From there, anything might happen. He could phone a car to pick him up, hide out in the woods, keep running in any direction. He appeared to be in good shape for his age. If he got away now, he might escape for good.

Eric wasn't about to let that happen. Vanessa had suffered too much because of this man—would continue to suffer fear and uncertainty as long as he ran free. Eric crouched on the edge of his tree stand. Sherman had a gun out, no doubt ready to defend himself if anyone caught up to him. The criminal ran along the length of the ravine, still following the deer trail—the same trail Vanessa's grandfather had built his tree stand to oversee. As long as Sherman continued along that path, he'd pass almost directly below Eric.

Staying frozen still to avoid being seen, Eric watched Sherman's approach. He could see the man's face clearly— the man who'd conspired to hire Vanessa, then purposely sent Jeff to win her trust so he could kidnap her. The man who'd stolen eight years of her life.

Waiting until Sherman ran almost directly beneath him, Eric leaped down, shotgun in hand, catching the man by the back of his legs, bringing him down to the hard ground with a thump.

Sherman held tight to his gun in spite of being tackled, and pulled his gun arm around toward Eric. Just in time, Eric rammed him in the shoulder with the butt of the gun. Sherman's arm went slack, but he kept a hold on the gun while struggling to get up again.

Eric planted one hand on the man's shoulder and pivoted, swinging his legs around, bringing one boot down hard near Sherman's wrist.

The handgun slapped against the ground, but Sherman's fingers still clutched the handle.

Eric stomped again, ramming the gun free of the man's fingers, then kicking it away before planting one boot on his hand, pinning it to the ground, and dropping his opposite knee into the middle of the man's back. He gulped a breath and tried to think what to do next. An officer of the law would probably handcuff the man, but Eric had nothing to cuff him with.

Sherman's free arm flew back as if to strike at him. Eric swatted it with the shotgun, then pinned the hand to the ground with the barrel of the gun. He leaned into the instrument, causing Sherman to groan in pain.

"Don't try to get away," Eric cautioned him, still trying to think how he was going to bring the man in. Chances were, no one had seen Sherman run through the woods, and they were down in the ravine—easy to miss, in fact, impossible to see from the cabin.

Eric thought about removing his belt or his shirt and using it to tie Sherman's hands behind his back, but that would require letting go of the man. Could he hold the gun on him and march him back to the cabin? Surely Sherman would try to take back his own gun, or make a break for it, or fight him again.

"He was on the tree stand." Vanessa's voice filtered through the woods. "I don't know where—"

"I'm in the ravine!" Eric called out, twisting around as much as he could to see Vanessa and whoever she was speaking to.

A pair of figures appeared over the rim of the ravine.

"Freeze! FBI!" the man who was with Vanessa shouted.

Eric froze, one boot firmly holding Arthur Sherman's hand against the ground, his other knee planted in what he hoped was a particularly uncomfortable position against the criminal's spine, his gun holding the other hand pinned in the dirt.

The agent leaped down the side of the ravine, pulling out his cuffs and slipping one end around Sherman's wrist before Eric even let up with his boot.

Eric took a step back, waited just long enough to be sure the agent wasn't going to let Sherman wriggle free, and then reached for Vanessa.

She was trembling, one hand over her mouth as her eyes welled with tears. "You caught him? He came?"

Eric pulled her into his arms, pulled her tight to his chest, felt her still-pounding heart hammering against his and thanked God—that the men who'd taken everything from her had spared her life. That she was safe.

But Vanessa still seemed to be in shock as she absorbed the reality that Arthur Sherman had been caught—that indeed, even now, the FBI agent was shoving him back up the ravine, none too gracefully, on a forced march back to the cabin. "How did you— Where did he— How?"

"He was in the sedan. When the deputies circled the cars, he jumped out and ran for the woods, right along the deer trail through the ravine, which runs directly alongside your grandpa's tree stand." As he explained what had happened, they fell into step behind the FBI agent. Eric kept one eye on Sherman, just to make sure he didn't try anything. The agent had scooped up the criminal's gun, as well.

"You caught him." Vanessa seemed to finally accept that the situation was really true as she looked up at him with joy pooling in her eyes.

"Jumped on him from above and held him down until the agent got him cuffed," Eric explained, looking down at her with love rising in his heart, so grateful he'd had the opportunity to slay the monster for her, finally. To cut off the head of the human-trafficking ring and free Vanessa, finally and completely.

"Oh, Eric." Vanessa leaned against him as they walked back up the trail, her head nestled into the crook of his shoulder. "You caught him. It's over. They're all going to jail."

"They're all going to jail," Eric repeated. He couldn't resist planting a soft kiss on top of her head. He didn't want to rush her into anything—she'd been through so much—but he was so grateful for the opportunity to hold her. Finally.

She didn't seem to mind and nuzzled against his shoulder.

"It's over. You're free now."

"I'm free." Vanessa hardly sounded as though she could believe it. "Oh, thank God. I'm free." She let out a long, shaky sob against his shoulder. "I don't even know what to do."

"Well," Eric reasoned in a careful tone, "we're going to let your girls know everything is okay. And then, I understand you have a son you probably want to see."

"Yes. I need to see Sammy *and* Alyssa and make sure they're both okay. Arthur Sherman said something. Remember, I overheard him talking in Jeff's office building, something about keeping an eye on my sister and doing a job? But I don't know what a job is." She rubbed her eyes, looking exhausted as she tried to recall what she'd overheard.

Eric didn't like the sound of the phrase any more now than when Vanessa had mentioned it earlier. Were Alyssa and Sammy safe? Suddenly, he wondered if perhaps Vanessa should have called her sister the evening before, too. But now that the monster was caught, Alyssa and the baby should be safe, shouldn't they? How many arms could one monster have?

From what he'd known of this monster, too many. They needed to make sure Alyssa and Sammy were safe—and they needed to do so soon. "We'll head over there as soon as we pick up your girls. And then you could probably use some real sleep."

Vanessa sniffled and leaned back from him just far enough to look him full in the face. "I don't know. I don't even know *where* I can sleep. This isn't my cabin. I don't have anything. I don't even know—"

"Vanessa." He held her upright and leaned his face close to hers. "I know this is soon, and everything has happened really fast, but I want you to know—I'm here for you. I will be at your side as much as you want me there. Anything you need—a place to sleep, help getting your life back in order, whatever it is—I will find a way to make it happen. Unless you don't want me around."

"Don't want you around? Eric, I owe you everything. You caught the man who ruined my life. You risked everything. You're my only friend—you're all I have."

He couldn't help grinning broadly at her words. "You want me around?"

"Yes."

"Good. Because—I thought about telling you this years ago, but I was just a kid. Then you were gone, and I wasn't sure I'd ever get to say it to you. But you're okay, and now I can say it."

"Say what?"

Eric cleared his throat. "This is almost as terrifying as watching that gunman—" he started to confess, then changed his mind. "No, that was more terrifying. I need to tell you, I have loved you since we were teenagers."

Vanessa's mouth dropped open, and she looked at him with something like disbelief. "But I've been— I'm not— I'm damaged goods, Eric. I don't know if you know—"

"I know I love you. I know you're perfect, no matter what you've been through. No matter what those guys did to you—I know this. You're stronger than they are. They are going to jail, and you are getting your life back. You beat them. And I have nothing but respect and love for you."

Vanessa closed her eyes and a tear trailed down her cheek.

"That may have been more than you wanted to hear," he confessed. "I can back off, if you want me to."

"Don't back off." She looked up at him and, to his surprise, planted a kiss on his cheek. "It was exactly what I needed to hear. Thank you."

Eric turned to face her, his every instinct to press his lips to hers, but after all she'd been through, he wasn't sure if his kiss would be welcome.

Vanessa opened her mouth slightly, leaned closer, then her eyes widened, her expression questioning.

"I want to kiss you," Eric confessed in a whisper.

To his surprise, she grinned, then looked around the woods self-consciously. The FBI agent had led Sherman away. He could hear the agents in the cabin's front yard, but for now, he and Vanessa were still alone in the woods.

"May I?" Eric asked.

Vanessa gave him a look that was simultaneously eager and uncertain. "I'd like that," she whispered.

He intended the kiss to be little more than a whisper of

touch between her lips and his. But as he leaned in cautiously, as though she might break or—more likely—shy away if he moved too quickly, he breathed in the scent of her and felt the warmth of her breath, everything real about her that he'd missed all those years, staring at her picture on the missing-person posters.

He brushed his lips against hers, surprised when she leaned into him, extending the contact. He couldn't pull away then and wrapped his arms more snugly around her.

The kiss lasted several seconds—far longer than he'd intended. "You're sure you're okay?" he asked.

"That," she whispered, looking up at him with affection, "was good for me. Healing. Therapeutic."

After fearing she might not welcome his touch, Eric was thrilled to hear the kiss had had the opposite effect. "I would be more than willing to provide more...therapy," he told her, grinning as he gazed into her eyes.

"I'd really appreciate that," Vanessa told him honestly. She couldn't recall a time when she had ever felt so happy. Certainly not in the past eight years, or really, any time for a long while before that. So much of the spark of her friendship with Eric was still there, but there was a new, exciting chemistry between them she wanted to explore.

Eric beamed at her. "Good. Now, let's talk to these FBI guys and find out what we need to do so we can get going. We've got a family to put back together."

Vanessa smiled at him, overwhelmed, not just that she was finally free or even that they'd captured the men who'd held her captive for so long, but overwhelmed with affection for Eric and his determination to help her reunite her family. She couldn't wait to see her girls and baby boy again, or to see her sister.

But she also realized that their family was missing something—something it had never really had. Her kids needed a father. Not a kidnapper who kept them locked in the basement in fear, but a real father. Between the love and determination she saw on Eric's face and the promise in his words, she couldn't help hoping that he might be willing to fill that void in their lives, as well.

That was a question that would take time to answer, and she wasn't about to rush things. So much had happened so quickly, and there were plenty of details to attend to now. But for the first time in a long time, she felt hopeful for the future and excited about the days ahead.

And there was something else, too. Something she needed to say that she'd realized as she'd waited alone at the cabin. "Eric?"

"Yes?"

"I'm grateful for all your help and for your friendship. And I know I'm tired, and I've been through things that might make you doubt what I'm about to say, but I've also realized life is short, and you never know when you walk out a door if you'll ever walk in again, if you'll ever see the people you care about again and get a chance to say how you feel, so I'm going to say it." She took a long breath and looked into his eyes—eyes full of kindness and affection, an affection she'd craved for so long.

"I love you, too."

* * * * *

DANGER
IN THE MANGER

ONE

Alyssa Jackson knew all the sounds of the concrete statuary grounds because she'd grown up there, raised in the cottage that sat half-hidden behind the concrete beasts that crowded the yard like a cluster of woodland partygoers, frozen in time.

There was the chugging sound of the mail truck at 4:30—no, 4:45; he must be running late. The smooth purr of the local patrol car that came by every half hour or so from two to ten o'clock, five days a week. Only that one officer seemed to have her road on his loop. Maybe he was scoping out her fountains and lawn ornaments for a gift for his mother. Whatever his reason, he never stopped, and she rarely glanced up at the sound of his engine.

Then a long stretch of silence. No customers, as usual, not for a long time. The sun was almost set when finally, rising above the late-autumn chirrup of grasshoppers, Alyssa heard the all-too-rare sound of a potential customer coming to browse.

This evening it was a crunch of gravel under tires slowing to a stop. Alyssa had learned her response from her grandfather.

Don't look up.
Don't make eye contact.
Keep your head down, focused on your work, and only

*catch a glimpse of them, just in case they look impatient
and ready to buy—which almost never happens.*

*Give them time to browse, then slowly, casually, move
in. Don't scare them off by running up and trying too hard
to sell anything. These statues may be your livelihood, but
they are also your art, part of your soul. Don't seem over-
eager to part with them. Bargain hunters can taste desperation, and there's no sense losing money on a sale, no
matter how overdue the utility bill.*

The sound of a car door was followed by a shuffle of
footsteps—not the sound of approach. Whoever had pulled
up was lingering near their car.

Alyssa went inside. This customer might be shy, might
want a few moments to browse completely alone. Anyway,
Alyssa had the windows open to let in the rare warmth of
late October. She could hear if the customer needed anything, and she had work to do inside, too.

Footsteps. More footsteps, faster ones now. Then the
car door again. They were leaving?

That was fast. Maybe too fast. Alyssa darted outside
and saw a dark SUV down the street. It wasn't the hooligans again, here to steal the little lambs from her manger
scene right out from under the watchful concrete gazes of
Mary and Joseph, was it? They'd only ever come at night
before, but it was getting on toward evening now. Maybe
she could finally catch them.

Alyssa grabbed her phone from her pocket.

If it was the hooligans, she didn't want them to have a
chance to get away. She'd lost too many valuable statues
to their antics. She punched in 911 as she turned toward
the door.

A new sound wafted through the evening air.

A crying baby? That was a sound she didn't often hear.

Alyssa froze, one finger poised above the send button.
The patrol car had just swung by not five minutes before.

If he hurried, he could be back in a minute or two. This might be her only chance to catch the louts who'd been stealing her statues.

She heard the cry again. The sound completely threw her, coming, as it did, from where Mary and Joseph stood guard over the concrete manger. For an instant, she couldn't imagine why that sound would be in her yard at all.

Then she remembered an old email-forward warning. It was old, old news and so silly she'd hardly paid it any heed. Attackers—thieves, kidnappers, would-be rapists— would place a tape recording of a baby crying outside a single woman's home to lure her out, alone.

Were they trying that trick on her?

Alyssa pressed Send. Hooligans or would-be rapists, it didn't matter. The police should come, either way. She hoped they'd hurry. The crying-baby sound was unnerving. It sounded so real.

Chris flipped a tight U-turn in the middle of the street. He switched his flashing lights on to speed back to the concrete-statuary business.

Finally, an opportunity to check the place out. He'd kept it in his sights ever since the first report from the national wire. Drug residues in broken concrete statuary—but nobody knew the source. It looked like that local girl Alyssa Jackson's work. He'd never understood how she made a living off her business, but that hunch alone wasn't enough to warrant taking a closer look. It was just enough to keep him driving by on his regular patrol circuit in hopes that someday he might see something conclusive.

The dispatcher's words were confusing, though. Something about hooligans, missing statues and a crying baby? It was the baby part that seemed weirdest to him, but he'd know in a few short minutes what that was about.

He made the last corner onto the long, semirural road

on the edge of town and immediately saw the clusters of concrete figures that cluttered the sale yard. There were no vehicles nearby, just a Toyota Sequoia driving down the road, almost out of sight.

As Chris pulled into the gravel parking area, he saw a woman standing among the concrete statues in the yard.

Alyssa Jackson. Chris didn't actually know her. He only knew of her. She was the twin sister of that girl who'd gone missing right after he started work on the local police force. Vanessa Jackson. Chris would never forget her name or her face. She'd been the first big case he'd ever dealt with after joining the department, though as the junior member of the department, he hadn't been allowed to do more than support the work of those assigned to the case. Vanessa's sudden disappearance was still unsolved, and her pretty smile haunted him from the missing-person posters that had long ago been shoved to the back of the file drawers.

The sisters were supposedly identical twins, but while Vanessa had been unusually pretty, Alyssa was plain. The face that peered out from behind the screen door was devoid of makeup. Her dark hair was pulled back into a haphazard ponytail, and a couple of dusty smudges highlighted one cheek.

Chris threw the car into Park and hopped out. As he approached from across the far end of the half acre of concrete display yard, Alyssa weaved a path through the statues, going around the front of the house toward a pair of human figures whose gray faces bent nearly together.

Mary and Joseph. Chris recognized the nativity scene and trotted closer, leapfrogging a series of lawn toads and circling wide of a lineup of cast deer, a strange noise carrying through the evening air

Was that a baby crying? The sound seemed out of place, but the dispatcher had said something about a baby.

Chris reached Alyssa just as she bent her head over the manger, reaching for the bundle nestled amid the concrete hay.

"It *is* a baby," Alyssa murmured. She glanced back at Chris, her face full of confusion and wonder.

"A baby?" he repeated, though he was close enough now to see the child clearly. He looked around for any sign of the hooligans the dispatcher had also mentioned, but there was no one. The SUV he'd spotted in the distance was long gone, and Chris realized with regret he hadn't thought to note the plates.

"Whose baby?" he asked.

Alyssa only shook her head and fumbled with the latch that kept the baby buckled into the car seat that sat, safe and secure, in the deep well of the manger. The buckle snapped open, and she slid the straps from the infant's shoulders.

As she did so, Chris spotted writing on the front of the child's shirt. It looked like words, hastily scrawled with a marker on the cotton knit that stretched across the drum of the baby's full tummy.

"What does that say?" He took a step closer and reached for the baby as Alyssa carefully lifted the crying child from the seat.

"I don't know." Alyssa held the baby awkwardly, clearly unused to handling infants. She glanced about a second, then perched on the edge of the manger, propping the baby on her lap.

Chris was no expert on babies, but he had helped out quite a bit with his nieces and nephews while his brother-in-law was deployed in the army. This kid looked to be a little under a year old, maybe nine or ten months. Strong enough to sit upright on Alyssa's lap as she eased back the little jacket that obscured the message on his shirt.

Crouching in front of them, Chris held the shirt flat enough to read the words.

A DNA test will prove this is Alyssa Jackson's son.

He read the message out loud, then looked up at Alyssa. Her brown eyes widened.

"I don't—" she started, then blinked and held the baby backward at a slight angle, staring into his face, her expression incredulous. She squinted at his face, then looked up and all around, as though half expecting someone to appear from behind a statue.

Chris took in everything, the messages sharply conflicting. Alyssa didn't appear to know how to hold the child. She didn't seem familiar with him at all. Nor did her slim, wiry figure at all resemble the post-baby pudginess his sister had fought back for years before regaining something of her prebaby figure. Not that all women gained weight after having a baby, but still, Alyssa simply didn't look or act like a mother.

Moisture sprang to Alyssa's eyes, but she pinched her lids shut, pulled the baby close to her chest and planted her lips against the downy softness of his fuzzy head.

Unsure what to make of this call, Chris rocked back on his heels. Whatever his hopes of finding evidence of drug smuggling, they took second place to this strange case. The woman before him held the baby close, and the child's cries stilled. The baby reached for a lock of her hair and pulled her ponytail into worse lopsidedness, but Alyssa didn't even open her eyes.

Chris looked around. There was still no sign of anyone else nearby. Mary and Joseph looked blankly down at the scene in the manger, their faces frozen in blissful serenity, as though they were pleased with what had just unfolded. Chris didn't feel nearly so joyful about it.

"Is this baby your son?" he asked, though he felt certain of the answer. He'd been driving by this place for over a year. Alyssa Jackson had never looked pregnant. She'd never stopped lugging heavy statues and bags of cement mix around, as a pregnant woman probably should have when her due date neared and after giving birth. He'd never seen any sign of a baby around here before, and he felt certain he'd have recognized her name had it appeared in the births section of the local paper.

Alyssa opened her eyes but didn't take them off the baby. She stared at his face in silence for a moment. The little boy's eyes watched her in wonder. She offered the baby a tentative smile.

He returned a smile that was equally unsure.

The two seemed to appraise one another.

No, this wasn't a meeting of two familiars, but a first-time introduction. Chris could feel it, would testify to it under oath if he was ever called to do so.

Alyssa didn't take her eyes off the baby. Her smile grew. "A DNA test will say this is my son."

TWO

Alyssa stared at the baby, her thoughts racing. A DNA test. Yes, of course. She and her sister had shared a rare mutual thrill when they'd learned in biology class that as identical twins, their DNA was the same. Genetically, Alyssa could pass for Vanessa, and vice versa, not that they'd had any reason back then to use that knowledge for any purpose.

That discovery had come mere weeks before a far more tragic occurrence. Vanessa had gone to work, as usual, at The Flaming Pheasant restaurant near the interstate. Alyssa had heard her car pull away from the house where they lived with their grandfather, just as she'd heard her sister leave for work so many dozens of other times. But she'd never heard her return.

Vanessa had been missing for eight years. She'd been declared legally dead, and Alyssa had relinquished all hope of ever seeing her again.

But if, as the words scrawled on the baby's T-shirt claimed, a DNA test would prove Alyssa was the little boy's mother, it could only mean one thing.

The baby was her identical twin sister's son.

Vanessa was alive.

Chris stared at Alyssa, who refused to look at him, much less meet his eyes.

He didn't like being lied to. Unfortunately, as a police

officer, he got lied to a lot—so much so that he'd developed an acute sensitivity to lying, a sort of built-in lie detector that sent the hairs on the back of his neck standing on end whenever someone tried to pull one over on him.

And those hairs were all prickling straight out now.

He doubted Alyssa had ever seen this baby before, certainly not recently. Just as he was nearly positive she hadn't given birth any time in the past year.

He took a step back and considered his next move. The dispatcher had sent him to investigate claims of hooligans, stolen statues and a suspicious crying sound. And he still hoped to get a look around, to learn if his drug-smuggling suspicions were justified. But the woman in front of him was, at best, emotionally volatile. He knew from experience that trying to get between a mother and her baby was as dangerous with humans as it was with bears and wolves.

Not only was she probably lying to him, but there was every chance the woman in front of him was crazy, too. He'd have to proceed with caution if he expected to stick around long enough to investigate anything.

Alyssa gazed at the baby's face in pure wonderment. Yes, she could see the resemblance clearly now, to her baby pictures as well as her sister's. There was every chance this little person was her own flesh and blood, but how had he ended up in her manger?

When Vanessa had disappeared eight years before, there had been plenty of theories about what might have happened to her. Some suggested she'd run away—but Alyssa doubted that. No matter how difficult things were in their nontraditional household, twin teenage girls being raised by their grandfather, Vanessa hadn't been that unhappy. A little morose at times. And she'd grown increasingly distant from Alyssa, but they still shared important things.

Vanessa wouldn't have run away, not without her car

out of her head. Vanessa clearly wanted to keep the baby safe, maybe even hidden.

Which meant Alyssa needed to get rid of the police officer in her yard as quickly as possible. The last thing she wanted was to draw attention to the child's presence. Just as she began to wonder how to get rid of him quickly, the officer spoke.

"You called 911 to report suspicious activity. Do you want me to have a look around?"

"No!" Alyssa nearly yelped. Then, since the police officer looked startled, she tried to make her voice sound casual. "That's really not necessary. Everything's okay, I guess. Sorry to bother you."

The policeman stared at her with slightly narrowed eyes, and Alyssa returned his look. She'd been so distracted by the baby, she hadn't really noticed anything about him. Now she realized he was youngish, maybe even still in his twenties, not much older than she was. Standing above her as she sat on the edge of the manger, he seemed impossibly tall and broad-shouldered, intimidatingly so. She might have considered him handsome if he hadn't been glaring at her so warily, his posture indicating he had no intention of going anywhere yet.

Fear trickled through her veins, more acutely now than when she'd dialed 911. Too late, she wished she hadn't called at all. Sure, it would have been nice to catch the hooligans who'd been stealing the concrete lambs from beside Baby Jesus's manger, but obviously, this baby wasn't related to her missing concrete statues.

Now she needed to be rid of the policeman. The baby on her lap whimpered, and, fearing he might be about to cry again, she bounced her knee.

He burst into a loud sob.

Alyssa looked down at the child, wishing he'd calm down so she could deal with the police officer. But the baby was only getting started. His cries grew in volume, and his face began to turn red.

"Shh," she soothed near his ear, but his cries were so loud, she doubted he could hear her.

"Are you sure this is your baby?" the policeman asked.

Alyssa bit her lip and looked down at the red-faced tyke, wishing she knew how to calm him or what to say. What had Vanessa been thinking, leaving the baby without any words of instruction, without even showing her face? Did her sister need her to pass the child off as her own? What would happen if she admitted the truth?

"He's my—" Alyssa started, struggling to be heard above the child's incessant wailing. She glanced up at the officer's withering glare.

He didn't believe her, did he?

And wasn't it illegal to lie to a police officer, even if, technically, a DNA test would conclude she was the baby's mother? Never mind that she hadn't really lied. And her sister had started it. She certainly couldn't take the deception any further.

The man crouched down to her level again and extended his arms toward the child. Alyssa looked at the wailing baby and then at the officer.

"You're not going to take him away from me—"

"I'm just offering to hold him until he calms down." The man had to nearly shout to be heard over the baby's angry cries.

Alyssa handed the child over, wondering if perhaps the infant knew she had no clue how to care for a baby. Perhaps he could sense her inexperience and was instinctively concerned for his own well-being.

The officer held the baby against his shoulder and patted his back while bouncing ever so slowly up and down.

The baby's cries stilled. He burped, looked a little startled and then smiled.

Alyssa felt more than a little frustrated. Her sister maybe wasn't dead after all, had left her a nephew she didn't know she had and now the baby liked the policeman more than he liked her. "How did you do that?"

"It sounded like a gassy cry. You probably dislodged an air pocket when you bounced him on your knee, and it was causing him pain. The bobbing helps the bubbles rise. It relieves the pain and makes him happy again." The man made an expression that was more of a kind smile than a satisfied smirk.

Alyssa tried to decide whether the officer could be trusted. Smiling now, the guy looked deceptively nice. Even handsome. Not that she was at all noticing.

No, she needed to get rid of the policeman and take the baby inside, out of sight. Maybe she should go into hiding. The policeman had to go.

But he had managed to calm the baby. She had to give him points for that. And she couldn't lie to him—not only did it go against her principles, but it would surely get her into trouble.

"So…" The officer raised an eyebrow and gave her a conspiratorial half grin that raised a dimple on one cheek.

Okay, so the man was sincerely good-looking.

"Whose baby is this, really?"

Alyssa opened her mouth and tried to think how to form a response.

The officer spoke first. "I don't believe he's yours. You don't seem to know him, and he doesn't seem to know you."

"I think he may be my sister's baby."

"Your sister?"

Was it her imagination, or did the policeman go a little pale?

Chris stared at Alyssa, unsure what to make of her words. It had been several years since her twin sister had gone missing, but Chris still recalled the basics of the case. The twins had lived in the little cottage behind the statuary yard, together with their grandfather. They had no other family that he'd ever heard of.

"What sister?" Chris asked, continuing to slowly bounce up and down, keeping the child soothed with the motion.

Alyssa looked up at him uncertainly, and Chris saw it clearly now, the resemblance to her attractive twin sister. Alyssa was older than the dated photo on all the missing-person posters, but the resemblance was still unmistakable. Vanessa's eyebrows had been plucked into slender arches, while Alyssa's were natural. And while Vanessa's eyes and lashes had stood out due to the makeup she wore, Alyssa's eyes were still warm and brown and pretty. Her whole face was very pretty.

It took him a little by surprise, because he'd driven past so many times, watched her working in her grubby jeans and stained work shirts, her hair always pulled back efficiently in a ponytail. It had never occurred to him that close-up she might be perfectly attractive.

But even more than her physical attractiveness, Chris was struck by the uncertainty in her expression, the pursed-lip pensiveness. She was clearly weighing whether she ought to trust him.

Funny, he'd been asking himself the same question about her.

She began pensively, "I was born with an identical twin sister. We share the same DNA."

Chris stopped bobbing. Time seemed to still as he stared at Alyssa, seeing the face of her sister from the missing-person posters, seeing time swirl between them. Vanessa Jackson had been declared legally dead long before, way too long ago to have a baby as young as the child he held in his arms. Unless...

"Your sister, Vanessa?" Chris figured he must have misunderstood. He had to have misunderstood. If Vanessa had a child, that meant she was still alive or had been alive recently. It meant she was still out there, even though they'd never found her. It meant the case that had been closed when she was declared legally dead ought, by rights, to be opened again.

It meant he'd failed—failed to find Vanessa, filed the case away in the wrong drawer, closed the search while she was still out there to be found.

But Alyssa's face brightened, however slightly. "You've heard of her?"

Heard of her? He'd prayed for her safe return. Words seemed insufficient to explain how he knew her, since he'd never actually met her. But he knew details about her life and disappearance, more details than he knew about plenty of other people he called his friends. He nodded. "She went missing—"

"Eight years ago."

"Eight years ago," Chris repeated, remembering. He'd been on the force just over eight years, ever since he'd graduated from the law-enforcement academy. Vanessa's disappearance had been his first big case. "But she was declared—" he dropped his voice to a whisper, unwilling to speak the words too loudly in the presence of the child, even if the baby was too young to understand "—legally dead."

"I know." Alyssa's face pinched tight for a moment, as though she was fighting back tears or some awful memory. She reached for the baby and drew his jacket to the side so the hastily scrawled message showed clearly. "But if a DNA test would prove this is my child, what other explanation is there? Identical twins share the same DNA. I don't have a child. If he carries my DNA—"

Chris thought of another possibility, however slim. "You've never sold your eggs, for example, to a fertility clinic?"

"No. And I've never…" She looked uncomfortable. "I've never had a child. Or been pregnant."

"Right." Chris cleared his throat. "Nobody ever figured out what happened to your sister, did they?"

"There was never any sign of her. One of the cooks saw her walk out the rear employee door of The Flaming Pheasant. That was the last time she was seen." Alyssa extended one hand toward the baby, who grasped her finger.

"So she was declared dead based on—"

"Based on the fact she'd been gone so long, with no sign of her ever turning up anywhere, and foul play suspected in her disappearance." Alyssa bit her lip again and looked from the baby's face to Chris and back again. She let out a long breath. "I still suspect foul play. Not just in her disappearance, but—" She shook her head. When she glanced up at him again, her eyes were moist. "She always wanted to be a mom. Always. She dreamed of it. I always wanted to run the statuary business. We used to joke that she got the mothering gene and I didn't—even though we share genes, obviously. But for her to leave her baby with me—" Alyssa shuddered.

"The foul play," Chris suggested, his voice purposely soft, not wanting to disturb the baby or Alyssa, "whoever took her. You think they're still—"

"They're still controlling her, or holding her prisoner or whatever it is. Maybe she escaped just long enough to hand off the baby? She wouldn't be parted from her son unless his life was in danger. And hers, I suppose. Why else would she go eight years without letting me know she was alive, unless she had no other choice?"

Chris watched the woman wrestle with all the horrible possibilities and wished he had something reassuring to tell her. But he could still hardly wrap his head around the idea. Was Vanessa Jackson still alive? And she'd left her son in her sister's manger? It seemed a bit crazy, but Chris had to admit, the little tyke in his arms bore a strong resemblance to his aunt. And Vanessa's body had never been found, so it was technically possible she was still alive, no matter what the legal record said.

His mind now made up, Chris was ready to take the next step toward finding Vanessa Jackson. He may have failed her before, but if she was still out there, he could find her. "We need to file a report about this baby and get your sister's case reopened."

Alyssa took a sudden step back and looked up at him as though he'd slapped her. "No. That's the last thing we should do."

THREE

Just as she'd been about to start trusting him, Alyssa was reminded that this police officer, no matter how charming his smile, was a stranger, an unknown entity. And just like the incompetent officers who'd failed to find her sister eight years ago, even going so far as to suggest she and her grandfather had pushed Vanessa to run away, this man was more likely to hurt than help her.

She'd also thought of something else. Surely her sister knew better than to leave the baby with her without any instructions. Vanessa had always been the twin who was good with kids—Alyssa had been better with cement mix. Like the note on the baby's shirt, perhaps Vanessa *had* left more instructions. Alyssa just needed to find them. She could check the car seat, the diaper bag, the rest of the baby's clothes.

And really, she needed to get the kid indoors. Not only was the evening growing dark and cooling off, but if Vanessa had left the baby there to hide him, Alyssa wouldn't be doing her sister any favors, either, standing outside in plain sight from the road.

"I'll take him." She held out her hands toward the baby, whom the officer still held upright in his arms. "I need to get him inside."

"I can carry him in for you."

Alyssa watched the man's face as he spoke. Was he

just offering to be friendly? There almost seemed to be a hint of challenge in his words. His steely gaze didn't leave her face.

She weighed her options quickly. She wanted to get the baby inside, perhaps even more desperately than she wanted rid of the officer. And the man *did* seem to have a knack for handling the kid. He knew about gas bubbles, anyway, which Alyssa had no clue about. Perhaps it would be easier in the long run, if she let him carry the baby inside. He could hold her nephew while she searched for further instructions from her sister.

And if Vanessa needed help, it might not be a bad idea to have the law on her side. Granted, the officers who tried to find her sister eight years before hadn't been much help. Their efforts had certainly been disappointing.

But there was something about this man that made her almost wish he could help her.

"Okay," she agreed. Then, for good measure, she added, "Thank you. I'll carry the car seat and the diaper bag."

"You sure you can handle both of those?" the policeman asked as Alyssa hoisted up the bulging bag and awkward car seat.

"Portland cement comes in ninety-four-pound bags," she informed him. She lifted the car seat high enough to avoid bumping it into any of her statuary as she led him to the front door of the cottage. "I carry those around all the time." As she spoke, she paused and set down the car seat on the front stoop to free up her hands to open the door.

The officer let out a low whistle.

"What?" Alyssa glanced around the yard but didn't see anything in the twilit darkness. Granted, with so many statues clustered around, anyone could be hiding close by without her seeing them.

"That's a lot for a girl to lift."

Alyssa felt her face color and hoped the officer couldn't see. Yes, she had always been the tomboy, the athlete—

of the dimple and to get to work figuring out what her sister must have been thinking, leaving her a child. Really, she needed to get out more. At what point had she been reduced to muttering aloud?

Not until Officer Jensen showed up.

She shook off that thought and went to work, unzipping the main compartment to reveal diapers—no messages anywhere on or amid those that she could see—wipes, a couple of outfits, a small blanket, a can of baby formula, an empty bottle, pacifier, and a few adorably tiny hats and socks.

The closest thing she could find to instructions was the printed label on the side of the formula can.

Mix four level scoops with eight ounces of water.

Not any more complicated than mixing cement, as it turned out. But it didn't help her figure out what her sister was up to—or more important, how to help her.

Alyssa felt her sense of desperation increasing as she checked every pocket in the bag. Tissues. More wipes. Another empty bottle.

Nothing personal or handwritten, no clues that would tell her anything about her sister's whereabouts.

Officer Jensen eyed the empty bottle. "I wonder how long it's been since he ate."

"I don't know. How often do babies eat?"

"At this age? Probably every three to four hours. Since we don't know when he ate last, he may be due for supper soon."

"Supper." Alyssa repeated the word flatly. She hadn't eaten anything yet herself, not that she often stopped work until close to bedtime. There was always too much to do. But a panicked thought occurred to her. "What do babies eat at this age? More than just bottles?"

"Oh, sure." Officer Jensen squinted at the baby's face.

moved it out of the baby's reach. "I think this little guy is getting hungry. What else do you have?"

Alyssa bent to inspect the contents of the fridge. Ketchup. Eggs. A couple of lemons and half a head of cauliflower. Nothing that looked like baby food.

"Do you have any applesauce?" The officer peered in beside her, munching the cookie and holding the rest away from the infant's grasping fingers.

"Sorry."

"Oatmeal?"

"Yes. Babies eat oatmeal?"

"My sister's did—with applesauce. But I think plain should work, too."

"Okay." Alyssa gulped a breath and stuck her head in the cupboard, hoping the officer hadn't spotted the tear that sneaked down her cheek. She wiped it away quickly. She was not a crying person, generally. It took a lot to make her cry. Like the disappearance of her sister.

Or the fact that her sister had been close enough to leave her child behind but hadn't stuck around long enough to see her or leave any explanation about where she'd been for the past eight years.

Chris finished off the cookie and stood back while Alyssa made the oatmeal. He still wanted to look around, maybe even check out the workshop to see if he could find anything that would point to the drug-smuggling operation he'd read about, but for now he had plenty of reasons for simply observing Alyssa.

For one, if she was related to the drug-smuggling operation, maybe she would do or say something that would give herself away. He also wanted to be sure she could handle taking care of the baby before he left her alone with the child. He'd investigated enough child-neglect cases to feel a strong sense of responsibility toward making sure Alyssa knew what she was doing.

Granted, she certainly seemed to care about doing her best to take care of the child. The only thing he could really hold against her at this point was his suspicion about smuggling, and he had no evidence to back up those suspicions...yet. Alyssa had every legal right to care for her nephew if her sister had indeed placed the child in her care.

But she also clearly had no experience with babies, and she seemed to be overwhelmed by her nephew's sudden appearance.

Not that he blamed her. More than anything, the thought that filled his head was the real possibility that Vanessa Jackson wasn't dead. That she might be alive, somewhere nearby, even. That he could find her. Close the case. Give her family—well, her sister, anyway—some peace after all these years.

He'd watched Alyssa carefully as she unpacked the diaper bag, hoping Vanessa had left a clue to her whereabouts. But as Alyssa had emptied everything from the bag onto the desk, Chris had found himself more fascinated by Alyssa than the contents of the bag. The young woman was clearly wrestling with the sudden appearance of her nephew and all its implications. The possibility that her sister might be alive—and needing help, if only with taking care of her son—had dredged up powerful emotions.

Chris wanted to help and to stick around long enough to make sure both Alyssa and the baby were going to be okay. That was part of why he'd become a police officer in the first place—to help people, to see justice achieved. The fact that the first major case he'd encountered after joining the department had never really been solved still rankled him. But if they could find Vanessa, he could solve the case.

"Oatmeal," Alyssa announced, stirring the concoction. "It's still pretty hot."

"Let's mix up some formula. You can pour some into the oatmeal. That will cool it off."

"Got it." Alyssa stepped past him in the narrow kitchen, grabbed the formula can and the clean empty bottle, and stepped past him again on her way to the sink.

Her ponytail was still woefully lopsided, and she still had that smear of gray on her cheek, but she didn't look bad or silly. In fact, the way the loose hairs framed her face, it was as if she had one of those fancy hairstyles like models and famous people wore. She looked nice. Unpretentious. The kind of girl a guy could be himself around, whom he wouldn't mind spending time with and getting to know better.

What was he thinking?

For months, he'd suspected she might be smuggling drugs. He shouldn't get distracted by how easy it was to spend time with her. Even if she did make delicious cookies.

"Uh, here." He settled the baby back into the car seat as Alyssa finished mixing the bottle. "You can use the car seat for a high chair for now. I'm going to take a look around."

Alyssa looked up at him with fear in her eyes. "Look around?" She glanced about the tiny kitchen warily, as though danger might be lurking behind the refrigerator.

"You said you thought your sister was on the run? Or maybe escaped briefly from her captors?"

"You think there might—"

"I'm just going to take a look around. Okay?" Chris wasn't sure how well he could tie his excuse to her sister's disappearance, but he'd waited too long for this opportunity to let it pass, no matter how terrified Alyssa looked at the thought that danger might have followed her sister and the baby. He felt a twinge of guilt. "I'll come back inside when I'm done. Give a holler if you need me, okay?"

Chris stepped outside and took a deep breath of the evening air. It was dark out now, completely dark. This far on the edge of town, streetlights were few and far between. Alyssa's statues cast sprawling shadows in the moonlight. Chris stared at them for a few long seconds, but saw no sign of movement.

Ignoring the statues, he hurried to the workshop, fully expecting an automatic light to come on as he approached, but nothing happened. But then, the place looked pretty run-down. Used up. Old.

Just like the tiny cottage he'd exited, the workshop looked old. Though the front office and tiny kitchen had been spotlessly clean save for a couple of dishes in the sink, the carpet and linoleum had to be decades old. The cupboards were freshly painted but original to the house.

Chris tried the workshop door and was almost surprised to find it wasn't locked. But then, Alyssa had said she'd been busy working when the baby's arrival surprised her. She'd probably been coming and going between the workshop and the office and hadn't had an opportunity to close up for the night.

A tiny glow-in-the-dark ball dangled from a pull string. Chris caught it in one hand and gave it a tug. The lone bulb above clicked on, and he blinked in the sudden light.

A woodstove in one corner lay dormant, no cheery fire flickering in its window, though from the warmth of the room, Chris guessed there had been a fire burning earlier, probably during the cool morning. Near the stove, a battered old living room chair was nearly hidden by a couple rows of large shelving units crammed with molds of various sizes, each labeled with marker on masking tape. Chris gave a few a shake, but they all seemed to be empty, and it might take an hour to root around and check them all.

He turned his attention to the large workbench that stretched along one wall, where a number of molds lay open, ready to receive cement. They glistened slightly, and Chris realized they'd been greased with a lubricant from a tub on the counter, something to help the molded statues pop free easily once they'd set.

Just as Alyssa had reported, her work had been interrupted. She hadn't gotten her statues cast yet, though when he peeked under a damp cloth draped across a wheelbarrow, he discovered wet cement.

He felt a sudden pang of guilt. Alyssa had been about to cast the statues. If she didn't get them poured that evening, the concrete would probably harden too much overnight, and she'd have to throw it out. He didn't know a lot about cement, but he'd helped pour a few sidewalks over the years. Enough to know Alyssa hadn't been expecting a baby to show up in her manger that evening. She'd dropped everything when he did.

Chris poked around the workshop a little longer, but he found no evidence of drugs, even if the little lamb statues that sat at the foot of Alyssa's manger did closely resemble the fragments with the drug residue in the police report from Pennsylvania.

It was because of the lamb statues that he'd paid attention to the reports, recognizing the figures from Alyssa's display yard. From what he'd read in the reports, investigators had concluded that smugglers placed the drugs inside the statues while the cement was still drying in the mold. Then, with the drugs completely hidden, encased in concrete, they were free to ship the statues anywhere they wanted, transport them across state lines, and no one would ever suspect they were anything more than decorative art.

He circled the room one last time, nearly passing by the woodstove and overstuffed chair before he noticed a door behind them, painted the same ancient smudged white as the walls. A second room, half-hidden out of sight? He grabbed the knob, surprised when it wouldn't turn in his hands, especially considering how easily he'd entered the door to the building. This far from the lone ceiling bulb, shadowed by the shelving units thick with molds, it was difficult for Chris to see much, but the knob looked newer and had a keyhole.

In a place where nothing else was new or locked, Alyssa had put a locking knob on an interior door. Why?

To hide a drug-smuggling operation? Chris couldn't know, not without gaining access to the other side.

The one thing Chris did discover with any certainty was that Alyssa didn't spend much money. Her truck was old, her house and belongings small and dated, and even her workshop lacked any sign of new purchases, save for the shiny doorknob. Given that Alyssa clearly took care of her things and kept them neatly organized and, in the case of her freshly painted kitchen cabinets, updated in a thrifty manner, Chris felt certain she'd have made updates if she had the funds.

Drugs made money. Lots of money. And Alyssa didn't appear to have any.

Maybe his theory was incorrect. But those little lamb statues looked so similar to those reassembled from the fragments of the statues that had been used to smuggle drugs.

If only he could access the room beyond the little door. Chris glanced about, hoping to spot a key, but a sound cut through the night, calling all his attention away from the door.

The baby was wailing. Loud, angry cries—more upset than his discontented bawling before.

Chris realized he'd left Alyssa and the child essentially alone. He all but leaped over the overstuffed chair as he ran for the back door of the house, praying everything was okay, that the young woman and her nephew were safe.

FOUR

Alyssa looked up as the police officer surged through the back door and felt an unfamiliar mixture of fear and relief roll over her. Fear because the officer looked alarmed. Relief because she didn't know how to make the baby stop crying, and it scared her.

"What's wrong?" Officer Jensen crossed the room in two strides and crouched in front of the baby, who now sat perched on her lap screaming furiously.

"I don't know." Alyssa had to shout to be heard over the baby's cries. "He ate the oatmeal just fine, and I thought he wanted to drink the bottle. He reaches for it and takes one gulp, then pushes it away. He just keeps screaming. Do you think he's in pain? Did I do something wrong? The oatmeal wasn't too hot—I checked it first."

The officer picked up the bottle. "Did you warm the bottle first?"

"Warm it?"

"If he's used to drinking it warm, he might not take it cold."

"No, I didn't warm it. I didn't know. Let's try that." Alyssa watched, helping when needed, memorizing the steps, as Officer Jensen heated water in a cappuccino mug, then placed the bottle in the warm water to heat indirectly. The baby watched them warily, his loud cries almost accusatory, as the policeman held out the warmed bottle.

"He probably thinks it's still cold," Officer Jensen explained as he nudged the bottle toward the baby's lips.

Glaring at them, the baby sucked once and started to push the bottle away. Then, with an expression of surprise that might have been humorous had Alyssa not just endured long minutes of his screaming, he settled in and drank steadily.

"There," Alyssa said, hardly believing the child could throw a fit over something so simple. "I had no idea."

"Taking care of babies can be complicated." Officer Jensen gave her a long look and cleared his throat ominously. "We have foster families that could—"

"What? No. You're not taking—" Alyssa felt instantly betrayed, but at the same time, vulnerable. True, she was utterly incompetent. But she was also the baby's only legally living relative.

"I'm just saying, I mean, for the child's welfare."

"No. No—I haven't broken any laws. I mean, I don't know what I'm doing, but I'll figure it out, okay? This is my sister's baby. He is all I have left—" Tears welled up in spite of her anger, and she hugged the baby close. For his part, the infant sucked contentedly at the bottle. Alyssa remembered that she needed to convince the officer to leave.

"Thank you for your help. Are you done checking outside? You didn't find anything?"

"There's a locked door near the woodstove in your workshop. Where's the key?"

"You can't go in there."

"I need to."

"No, you don't." Alyssa realized she should have gotten rid of him sooner. But it had been reassuring having him there. And he had figured out about heating the bottle, which had been a huge help. But now he definitely needed to go. "It's late. I'm sure you have a lot of things to do—"

"I need to file a report about this visit."

"No, you don't."

"Yes, I do. You placed a 911 call. I responded. I need to fill in the blanks about what I found. If we need to reopen your sister's case—"

Fresh fear surged through Alyssa. She had to make the officer understand. "Look, Officer Jensen, you've been a huge help. Really, you have, but I should never have called the police."

"But you *did*." The officer looked at her firmly, no hint of a smile on his face. If anything, he only looked that much more determined to fill out his report.

Alyssa had to make him understand. "My sister has been missing for eight years. Everybody thought she was dead, and now her baby shows up in my manger. What do you think is going on? All I can think is—she's in danger, the baby is in danger. She left him with me to hide him, to keep him safe, and if you fill out a report, what do you think is going to happen? Whoever's after her is probably watching. Maybe they know about me, maybe they followed her—I don't know what's going on. I just know I can't let you say anything about this baby to anyone. Filing a report would be the worst possible thing you could do."

The officer listened, his bluish-gray eyes studying her face as she spoke. When she finished, he hung his head, then sucked in a long, slow breath and looked at her again.

Alyssa felt a trickle of fear at how he might respond.

He spoke in a patient tone, his words slow, measured. "I responded to your call. I've been out here for close to an hour. The taxpayers deserve a report."

Alyssa fought to think of an honest answer that would satisfy the taxpayers without giving away to anyone what had really happened. "Say I panicked and called the police.

That much is perfectly true. I didn't realize I was supposed to take care of—of a relative's baby. Say it was nothing, a weird fluke thing."

"You want me to use the words *weird fluke thing?*" The officer's stoic expression broke, the words sounding absurd coming from his mouth. He cracked a smile, which she could tell he'd fought to suppress.

Alyssa could barely keep from giggling like a love-struck teen at the sound of those words coming out of the handsome officer's mouth. That and his dimple showed up again when he smiled. It was a good thing he didn't flash that too often, or she might not be able to think straight. And she was not a love-struck teen.

Whatever the case, it didn't change the fact that he needed to go, and she needed to carry on. She had a wheelbarrow full of concrete mixed and ready to pour, molds greased and ready to receive it. If she didn't get it done before she went to bed for the night, she'd have to start all over in the morning, and the wheelbarrow of concrete would be a total loss.

Not that any of that was as important as keeping the baby on her lap safe. The child had sucked the bottle dry, and it now made empty air sounds. Alyssa tugged it from his hands, and he grasped after it and began to whimper when she didn't give it back.

"Do you think I should make him more?"

Officer Jensen raised an eyebrow, which communicated, without words, a great deal of frustration. Alyssa realized she was consulting him, asking him for information. He'd already helped her, but she wasn't helping him. And she certainly didn't want to appear incompetent as a caregiver—not if he was still thinking foster care would be a safer place for the baby.

She stood. "I'll make him more." For an unsure moment, she juggled both bottle and baby.

or her favorite things, which Alyssa still kept in a trunk in their bedroom. She wouldn't have left without any sort of goodbye.

Which meant she may have been kidnapped. The Flaming Pheasant restaurant was on the interstate. People came and went on a regular basis. Anyone could have scooped up her sister and carried her off, but the odd thing was that there'd been no sign of her since. If she was still alive, wouldn't she have tried to escape?

It was that very question that had led Alyssa to request that her sister be declared legally dead—that and the fact that her grandfather's will had left everything to the two of them, and Alyssa hadn't been able to do anything with the property as long as it was tied up with her sister.

But if Vanessa had a baby, that meant she wasn't dead—or at least hadn't been dead until recently. Even the message on the baby's shirt, hastily scrawled though it was, appeared to be written in Vanessa's handwriting. So her sister had to be alive.

But surely she had to be in some kind of trouble to run off without showing her face, leaving her baby behind.

Alyssa made up her mind quickly. She didn't know what was happening, with her sister or the baby. But she knew one thing for certain: her sister had left the child for her on purpose, had composed the message on the baby's shirt specifically so Alyssa would be able to pass the child off as her own.

If Vanessa wasn't dead, she had to have a good reason for leaving her child behind, for sneaking away in silence in the first place.

What kind of reason?

Surely only a matter of life or death.

Alyssa hugged the baby close, grateful that he'd stopped crying and seemed comforted by being held on her lap, even if he seemed determined to yank a chunk of her hair

"I can do it," Officer Jensen offered.

Alyssa eyed him warily. Why was he being so helpful? She wasn't about to give him the key to her studio, no matter how nice he was. Not even if he flashed his dimple.

"You might want to burp that baby while I heat this up," the officer suggested.

Alyssa looked at the baby, a little unsure how to proceed. She tried patting his back lightly. It was a little like her statuary—she always rapped the molds feverishly or set them on a vibrating base to get the bubbles to rise. It was surprisingly similar with babies, but she didn't want to hurt him.

He chewed his fist hungrily.

"Try bouncing slowly, like I did," Officer Jensen advised as he dunked the bottle in hot water to warm it. "Just don't bounce him too hard, or he might throw up."

Tentatively, Alyssa stood, then bent her knees, dipping slowly before rising again. After a couple of dips, the baby let out a loud belch.

"He did it!" Alyssa felt a rare thrill. The bouncing worked. She'd done something right!

"Good job." Officer Jensen grinned as he handed over the warmed bottle.

Alyssa grinned back before she remembered that she needed to get rid of the policeman. "Thank you again for your help. Please don't say anything about the baby in your report."

"I'll be vague," he conceded. "Can I use the key to the door in your workshop?"

"No." Alyssa offered the bottle to the baby, who took it and began to suck contentedly.

"But what if—"

"There's no way anything having to do with my sister's disappearance could be in there. Sorry."

Officer Jensen hung his head in resignation. "Fine. But if you think of anything—"

"I'll call—" she began, then realized she most certainly wasn't going to do that, not if it might result in a written report.

The officer must have picked up on her uncertainty as her voice trailed off, because he offered, "I'll give you my cell-phone number. Where's your phone?"

Alyssa considered the offer for just a second before pulling her phone from her pocket and handing it over. It was a small concession that cost her little. She didn't *have* to call him. But if she needed his help, it would be nice to know how to get ahold of him.

"I put my number in under *Chris*. Call me if you need anything." He held out the phone to her.

"But after your shift ends—" Alyssa still held the baby, his eyelids sagging. She took hold of the phone and her fingers brushed Officer Jensen's hand.

Chris's hand.

"Call me anytime, day or night." He stressed the words, not letting go of the phone as he made eye contact with her, as though looking for some sign of confirmation that she would call him if she needed to, even if it was the middle of the night.

Alyssa felt the contact of his fingers. There was a connection between them, as though they were on the same team against the unseen foes who might be after the baby, as if they were parenting this child together.

She blinked away that thought. Maybe she needed to get out among people more.

"Anytime, day or night," she repeated. Only then did he let go of the phone. "Thank you, Chris."

Chris nodded and headed for the front door. Just before he let himself out, he turned to face her again. "I'll circle by several more times before my shift ends tonight and keep my eyes open for any activity. I'm glad your sister—" he swallowed, coughed, and Alyssa looked down at the baby who'd fallen asleep in her arms.

"I'm glad," Chris continued, "it looks like your sister is out there, still alive. I hope I can help—"

Words seemed to fail him again.

Alyssa offered him the best smile she could muster, fighting back all the other emotions that fought for dominance on her face. "Thank you for all your help."

Chris nodded silently and let himself out.

As the door closed silently behind him, Chris stood on the stoop and looked out across the statue-filled darkness, glancing especially long in the direction of Mary and Joseph and the little lambs clustered around their feet.

He was not an emotional guy. He hadn't cried since his own grandfather's funeral, and he'd been ten then. But the thought of what Alyssa was dealing with—the thought that Vanessa might still be alive, out there somewhere, running from something, so desperate she'd leave her baby behind...

Yeah, it was enough to make him a little emotional.

Chris walked back toward his patrol car, passing by the workshop again. Judging from the exterior of the building, the room behind the door was much smaller than the main area, with all its equipment, storage and workspace. But it was bigger than a closet, a full room in its own right. There was only one window that he could see, but someone had propped a sheet of plywood in front of it from the inside, completely blocking the interior from view.

Alyssa really didn't want him to see what was in that room. Why not? Because she was hiding evidence of a drug-smuggling operation? Based on what he'd learned about her so far, he was starting to doubt it. But if not that, then what?

* * *

Alyssa placed the sleeping baby in the car-seat carrier and draped his little blanket across his lap. Was he really going to sleep? She felt exhausted, emotionally drained by all she'd learned. Maybe the baby was tired, too.

But if he was willing to sleep, Alyssa wasn't about to waste a moment. The concrete she'd mixed up late that afternoon would be starting to cure already. She needed to get it in the molds as soon as possible, but she didn't dare leave the baby alone in the house, not if there was any chance somebody might be looking for him. She didn't want him out of her sight for even a second.

Lifting the car seat with both hands, she headed outside into the darkness. How many hundreds of times had she made this trek from back door to workshop in the dark without even thinking about it? She didn't need light—she knew the path by heart.

But tonight, even the familiar shadows of her statues sent a shiver up her spine. Had Vanessa really been here, if only long enough to drop the baby in the manger? Or had someone else come in her sister's stead? Either way, was it possible Vanessa's kidnapper may have followed her here? Was someone, even now, trying to track down the baby?

Alyssa couldn't shake the feeling that she was being watched.

Alyssa ducked into the workshop, placed the baby in his car seat out of the way near the overstuffed chair, and got to work filling her molds with mixed concrete and clamping them each shut in turn.

Then came the tricky part. In order for the sculptures to set correctly, they needed to be devoid of air bubbles. Normally, Alyssa would place them on the vibrating table that was made expressly for that purpose. But the device was horribly loud, and she had no doubt that if she turned it on, it would not only wake the baby, but terrify him, too.

And she was so glad he'd finally gone to sleep.

There was nothing else for it but to burp the statues by hand, one by one.

Alyssa picked up the first statue, a little lamb—one of her bestselling, original designs—and clamped a rag over the air-vent hole positioned at the top of the mold. The little lambs were molded upside down, so the blank space on top was actually the flat base at the bottom of the animal.

Covering the opening carefully, she shook the contents side to side. She didn't dare rap on the mold, either, because the noise might wake the baby. After several long minutes of shaking, she set the mold to the side, etched her artist's mark in the opening and started in on the next.

She'd finished three of the six when the baby awoke, his cries sounding pained, like the gassy cry he'd let out earlier. Alyssa had wondered if perhaps she ought to try to burp him after that second bottle, but since he'd fallen asleep, she'd hoped she was off the hook.

Scooping him up, she balanced him against her shoulder and patted his back.

He screamed in her ear.

She tried Chris's slow-bouncing maneuver.

The baby's sniffles subsided. But when Alyssa tried to place him back in his carrier, he started crying again. It quickly became clear that he didn't want to be put down. He was only happy when she did the slow bounce.

So Alyssa held the baby in one arm and a statue in the other, hoping the slow bouncing would be enough to burp the statues, too.

One by one, she bounced the statues and the baby, until her arms and legs ached from the effort. She'd already been emotionally exhausted by the long day and was now physically spent, as well. But even now, when she tried to place the baby back in his car seat, he started to cry.

She bounced again. His cries subsided, and she looked

around the room, her legs nearly wobbly with exhaustion. Her overstuffed chair beckoned to her from near the woodstove, and she pulled the chain to turn off the light before crossing the room to the chair.

Carefully, she eased herself down. The baby sniffled a little, but didn't cry.

Alyssa closed her eyes....

She didn't know how long she'd been dozing with the baby on her shoulder, when a noise awakened her. She froze, disoriented at awakening in the dark with her nephew drooling on her chest.

Had she really heard a noise?

Yes, and now there were more noises. Murmuring men's voices echoed from the other side of the shelving units. Alyssa couldn't see much beyond the physical obstructions, but she could tell whoever had entered—two men, if she heard the voices correctly—were carrying small flashlights. They kept the beams down, mostly pointed at the table where she'd placed her little lamb statues as she'd finished them.

For an instant, she wondered if perhaps Chris had returned with another officer, but the voices didn't sound like his, and from what little she could see of their potbellied silhouettes, they lacked his strong physique. Definitely not Chris, then. But who? The men were doing something with her statues. But what?

One stepped a bit to the side. Alyssa could see his profile against the backdrop of the moonlit window. He pulled back his jacket and fished for something in his inside pocket, but even as he did so, his flashlight illuminated everything that had been hidden by his jacket. His belt. A holster.

A gun.

FIVE

Alyssa froze, praying hard for her safety and that of the child who slept on her shoulder. So far, the men seemed oblivious to her presence, assuming themselves to be alone in the workshop. But if the baby awoke or made any noise, he could easily give them away.

Then what might happen?

Carefully, cautiously, she slipped her free hand into her pocket and wrapped her fingers around her phone. Should she call the police for the second time that day? She regretted the first call already. And she was in no position to answer the dispatcher's questions or even to talk at all. It was all she could do to hold tight to the phone, prepared to use it at her earliest opportunity.

Were these guys related to her sister's disappearance? They didn't seem to be looking for the baby—in fact, they seemed pretty focused on her statues. With their backs between her and the countertop, the men almost completely blocked her view of what they were doing, even if the shelving units hadn't been in the way.

The man had fished something from his pocket—a big bulging handful of something pale, almost shiny. It was simply too dark to see, especially with the full shelving units blocking most of her view. But she was grateful for the shelves because they kept her mostly hidden. As long as the men didn't shine their flashlights directly her way, and as long as the baby didn't make any noise, her presence might go undetected.

It wasn't until one of the men stepped to the side and bent over the countertop, a lamb form on the table in front of him, that Alyssa got a decent look at what they were up to. One of the guys used a slender object to do something in the air-hole opening at the top of the mold. Was he writing in the surface of the cement, much as she had placed her artist's mark there just before setting each mold aside?

But what was he writing? And why?

The men left as mysteriously as they'd arrived, sneaking out quietly and closing the door behind them. Alyssa waited several long seconds, listening carefully, trying to determine where they'd gone. Were they still around? She didn't hear a vehicle or anything beyond the first few quiet footsteps that faded quickly into the distance.

She didn't want to give away her presence by placing a phone call, but at the same time, if these guys were related to Vanessa's disappearance, or even if they were just the hooligans who'd been taking her baby-lamb figures, she wanted them caught. In order for that to happen, she couldn't let them get away.

Seeing and hearing no sign of them, she held her phone just high enough to see the screen and unlocked it deftly with her finger, making up her mind quickly to call Chris.

He answered on the second ring.

"Some guys were in my workshop. They had a gun," Alyssa explained in a hushed whisper.

"What? Where are you and the baby?"

"We're in the workshop. I think they're gone."

"I'll be right there. Stay on the phone with me, okay?"

"Okay."

Chris shoved his feet into shoes and threw on a jacket, then strapped his gun onto his ankle. If he was going to face somebody who had a gun, he needed to be similarly armed. His bedside clock told him it was just after midnight. What was Alyssa doing in the workshop—with the baby, no less—in the middle of the night?

Sneaking drugs?

Much as he might have thought so if he'd caught her at it the night before, after spending the evening with her, he was less sure. But one thing he knew with full confidence—the thought of her and that baby confronting armed men terrified him.

He raced to his garage, hopped into his Jeep and pulled onto the highway before lifting the phone to speak again. "I'm on my way. I'll be there in two minutes. You still okay?"

"Yes. I think those guys are long gone, but I never heard a car drive away."

"Maybe they parked at a distance, and I can still catch them."

He turned onto the long road, heavily shadowed by trees, and watched for any sign of movement or the glint of his headlights against the red glass of a vehicle's rear lights. But there was nothing, no sign of anyone.

Much as he'd have liked to pounce on anybody who'd dared trespass on Alyssa's property wearing a gun, he had no clue where to look. They could have gone in any direction.

No, far more urgently, he needed to get to Alyssa, to make sure she and the baby were safe. He slammed to a stop near the workshop, raising dust, bursting from his car and running at a dead sprint through the workshop door.

Alyssa stood from the overstuffed chair as he entered. She raised a silent finger to her lips, with a meaningful glance at the baby sleeping snugly against her chest.

For an instant, relief filled him, full and powerful, swelling inside him with foreign emotions. Alyssa and the baby were okay. More than that, they looked so peaceful and adorable together, the infant's head turned to the side, his chubby cheeks pink with sleep, his mouth slightly open.

Chris could have hugged them both.

Except, of course, he couldn't. He didn't even know them that well. It was just a huge relief that they were okay.

He stepped forward quietly, tugging on the light as he passed the glowing ball that dangled from the string. Alyssa met him near the workstation where her molds now sat in a cluster, filled and clamped, the smooth tops near their openings marked with a distinctive symbol etched in the exposed cement.

"That's my artist's mark," Alyssa explained. "It stands for Vanessa and Alyssa Jackson."

She traced the lines through the air with her finger, two overlapping *V*s turned at angles, forming something like an *A* with a *J* coming out the side.

Instantly, he recognized the symbol. It was identical to the marking on the fragments in the police report— the ones tainted with drug residue. They *were* the same lambs, then.

Chris felt the hairs on the back of his neck rising—his internal signal that someone was lying. Something didn't add up. He needed to find out exactly what was going on—and quickly, before the unfamiliar emotions Alyssa provoked in him clouded his judgment any more.

Alyssa whispered, explaining quickly, "After you left, the baby fell asleep, so I brought him out here while I finished the project I'd started earlier. But then he woke up and was fussing. I finally got him to calm back down, and then we both fell asleep in the chair. I woke up when I heard a noise. Two guys were standing over here, doing something with my statues."

Chris glanced over at the chair. It was mostly hidden behind the shelving units, but still, it couldn't be more than twenty feet away from where they were standing—where the intruders had been standing. He felt a jolt like fear at the thought. Fear and something worse.

Doubt.

Had Alyssa and the baby really been so close to mysterious intruders—who'd then disappeared completely by the time Chris rushed over? Or was she inventing a story to throw him off? Did she know he was onto her smuggling activities? Perhaps he shouldn't have pressed so insistently when asking to see what was behind the workshop door. But now he wanted to look inside more than ever.

The first step was to try to find a hole in her story. He'd gotten pretty good at questioning criminals over the years and could spot inconsistencies quickly. "What were they doing with your statues?"

"It was difficult to see. They had flashlights. One of them stood here." Alyssa planted her feet a step away from the countertop. "He took half a step back, pulled his jacket back and dug in his pocket." She demonstrated with her free hand, still holding the baby securely with the other. "That's when I saw the gun. It scared me. I was looking at the gun, and I didn't see what he pulled from his pocket, just that he had a bulge of something in his hand, and then he turned to face the table again and his back blocked my view."

"That's all you saw?"

"They were wearing gloves. I saw that much."

Chris ticked the point off on his mental checklist. Of course, gloves meant no fingerprints—a convenient detail if she was making up the story and needed to corroborate evidence. "Is that all you saw?"

"Right before they left, he stepped back again and bent close over the forms while the other guy held his flashlight pointed at the top. He was doing something—" She leaned over the forms and squinted.

"Anything look unusual?" As far as Chris could see, all six forms had identical slashes on top. "Do they look any different?" He scooted one closer so she could see.

Alyssa peered at the top, then looked startled. She scrunched her brows at him. "That's not how I draw it. I mean, it's close, but—they must have messed with it. But why break into my workshop in the middle of the night—" As her voice rose in pitch, the baby in her arms roused slightly, shifting his position.

"Shh," Chris whispered. The baby stilled while Chris said, "I have a theory. Do you mind if I check something?"

"Go ahead."

Chris grabbed a long, slender tool from the storage crock to his right and prodded the wet cement, stirring it in ever-deepening circles. The stick extended about a third of the way into the sculpture when he felt a solid mass. "Something's in there. A lump of some sort."

Alyssa shook her head. "The concrete was still smooth when I filled the molds. It dries from the periphery inward, not the other way around."

But Chris dug around silently while Alyssa protested. Finally, he fished out a plastic-wrapped packet coated in thick wet cement.

"What is that?" Alyssa looked sincerely surprised to see what he pulled from the form.

Chris studied her face an extra-long second, noting her response. Not too surprised, not enough to indicate she was faking a reaction. Just confused, quizzical. Honest? Maybe.

"Heroin," he stated with certainty.

She looked from the packet, its contents almost completely obscured by gray cement, to Chris, her expression disbelieving. "How do you know that? How can you tell? What would—"

"Shh," Chris quieted her again as the baby wriggled against her shoulder. He decided it was time to share what he knew—to watch her reaction in hopes of learning her degree of involvement. "I've seen reports of the drug being smuggled inside small concrete statues like your lambs. Law enforcement in Pennsylvania did a bust, but the criminals had already cleared out. They'd left in a hurry, though.

There was heroin residue on concrete statuary fragments in the trash."

Alyssa looked confused, maybe even a little sickened. "They broke the statues?"

"Drug smugglers at one end placed drugs in the statues before the cement dried. Then they shipped them to Pennsylvania, where the other end of the operation broke them open and took out the drugs. The statues provide a cover for the drugs, so they can ship them wherever they want without anyone realizing what they're really transporting."

"That is so wrong. But why break into my studio to do it? Why not just make their own statues?"

Chris watched Alyssa's face carefully, trying to remain objective in spite of how innocent and cuddly she looked with the sleeping baby snuggled against her shoulder. Her reaction seemed sincere, as if she didn't know anything about the drugs. Or did he just want to believe she was innocent?

Still, her question bothered him. Why would the smugglers go to all the work of breaking into someone else's place? It didn't make sense. That was why he'd assumed Alyssa was the real smuggler. But if she was really innocent, was someone trying to set her up? The question sent a shock of fear down his spine, far more than the usual prickles of suspicion.

Were drug smugglers targeting Alyssa?

He could see sincere fear in her eyes, so he played down the terror that had seized him. As casually as possible, he answered her question, "Maybe to point the finger of guilt away from themselves."

But Alyssa's face lit up with realization before he finished speaking. "That would explain my stolen lamb statues."

"What?" Chris latched on to the news. "When? How many?"

"I've had dozens stolen over the last few years. I always just assumed it was local hooligans playing around."

The explanation matched with what the dispatcher had told Chris when he'd been called out that evening. She'd even used the word *hooligans.* "Did you file a police report?"

"No."

Suddenly suspicious about her convenient explanation, which lacked support, Chris asked, "Why not?"

"It didn't seem like that big of a deal. The lambs aren't very expensive. The first time, I wasn't even sure I'd counted correctly. Then, when it happened again, I figured since I hadn't reported it the first time—"

Her excuse sounded flimsy. Now, more than ever, he needed to know whether she was innocent or guilty. He didn't want her to be guilty, but it was almost preferable to the idea that drug smugglers were trying to frame her. "Can I see what's behind that door?"

"You think the drug smugglers might have something back there?"

"I think somebody might," he answered truthfully.

Alyssa nodded, her eyes wide and trusting, though her cheeks looked noticeably flushed. Was she embarrassed? Was it a sign of guilt? She fumbled with one hand in her pocket, pulled out a ring of keys and sidestepped the chair on her way to the door.

Chris joined her in the small space, unwilling to allow her into the room first in case she might try to hide something before he saw it.

The door swung open, and Alyssa switched on the light. Chris stood in the doorway taking everything in, amazed and humbled by what he saw. When he looked down at Alyssa, he saw that she had her face buried amid her nephew's peach-fuzz hair, her eyes closed.

With a guilty, sinking feeling, Chris realized why Alyssa hadn't wanted him to see the room.

SIX

Alyssa was innocent.

Chris realized it all at once. He'd mostly thought it already, but the fact that she hadn't wanted him to see inside her studio had rankled him, a nugget of doubt he couldn't ignore.

But now he understood why she didn't want him to see. Unlike the commercial statues that crowded her sale yard, the statuary in this room was art. More than that, it was deeply personal. The room was filled with pieces that had been carved from concrete, apparently when it was in a partially dry state.

There was a statue of Vanessa and Alyssa as little girls, hand in hand. Another of them as teens, half facing one another as if through a mirror, though the girl on one side had turned away and was leaving, and the other looked after her, fingers grasping, unable to reach her, an expression of grief on her face. There were statues of an old man who must have been their grandfather, statues of abstract forms bending like light rays, a couple with two little girls, more statues than he could see or identify.

One caught his eye in particular. A young woman, probably Alyssa or Vanessa, sitting alone, hugging herself, her expression lonely and despairing.

Chris didn't know what to say. He cleared his throat. "These are amazing." He took a step toward a figure that was Alyssa or her sister. "Beautiful."

"See any sign of the smugglers?" Alyssa asked.

"Hmm?" Chris glanced around the room but saw only art. No, Alyssa hadn't been smuggling anything out of this room. The only reason she hadn't wanted him to see was because this room was full of her art. More than her art, it contained her heart, her deepest joys and disappointments, a side of her he doubted she let many see. "No, no sign of smugglers."

"But you didn't really look. You just— You— Oh."

Still captured by the amazing artwork around him, it took Chris a second to turn back to Alyssa. By the time he saw her face, it was too late for him to explain away what she'd clearly already realized.

Alyssa glared at Chris. He thought she'd been smuggling the drugs, didn't he? That was why he'd wanted to take a look around, why he was so interested in what was behind the door. He thought she was a criminal?

It made her feel sick. Worse than that, betrayed. She'd let him see inside her studio. She'd trusted him—maybe even started to think she ought to see more of him. Now she never wanted to see him again. "You need to go. Now."

"I found heroin in your statuary. I'm not going anywhere."

As the meaning of his words sank in, Alyssa felt her heart begin to pound so furiously, she feared it might wake the baby. The drugs were on her property. She couldn't prove they weren't hers. If she went to jail, what would happen to her nephew? What if Vanessa came back for him and he wasn't here?

Alyssa took a deep breath and tried to think. She felt light-headed. It had been hours since she'd had anything to eat or drink, just that one cookie, and she'd only had a bit of sleep. But what could she say that would convince him of her innocence? The intruders hadn't left behind any evidence that they'd been there—nothing but the drugs in her statue.

Chris spoke first. "Was the door unlocked when the intruders came in?"

"Yes. I was in here working. Then I sat down with the baby. I didn't realize I was going to fall asleep."

"Do you usually leave it unlocked?"

"During the daytime, yes, but then I'm coming and going all day long. Nobody could get in here without me noticing. And besides, I do most of my pours late in the day so they can dry overnight. And I lock my building at night."

"Always?"

"Yes."

"Your locks look as though they haven't been changed in a long time. Are there any keys to the locks unaccounted for?"

Alyssa closed her eyes and exhaled slowly, gathering strength to speak. "My sister had a set."

"Did her keys disappear with her?"

"Yes."

"So you had keys unaccounted for to your workshop—and your house?"

"Yes."

"And you never changed the locks? Whenever you have keys unaccounted for, you're supposed to change the locks."

Alyssa had wanted Chris to leave the moment she'd realized he suspected her of smuggling drugs. Now she wished even more that he was gone, that she didn't have to explain. "My sister had her keys with her the night she disappeared. How could I ever change the locks? What if she came back and needed in? I can't leave, you know. I can't sell this place and go away to art school to learn how to become a real sculptor. I have to be here for her." She hugged the baby closer. "She's coming back. She left her baby here. I'm not changing the locks, not until I can give her the new key."

At some point, as she was talking, the baby had begun to squirm. It wasn't until Alyssa gulped in air, trying to keep her emotions under control, that she realized her nephew was waking up. He wriggled in her arms. She moved to wipe her eyes.

Chris reached out a hand to help.

She wavered indecisively. Who was this man, this police officer, she'd come to trust so quickly? He wasn't really trustworthy, was he? He didn't trust her. He thought she was working with the smugglers. Was he the same guy who'd been driving past her place every half hour for the past year or two? Undoubtedly.

She wished he'd never come here at all.

And yet, as the baby squirmed against her, she realized she needed Chris's help. It wasn't something she wanted to need, but that didn't change the fact that he knew more about the baby, more about the smugglers and drugs, more about all the craziness in her life than she did right now. For all the things she'd handled alone in the past six years since her grandfather's death—bills, taxes, funeral expenses, even loneliness itself—this was a battle she sensed she couldn't fight alone.

Chris met her eyes with an uncertain understanding that mirrored what she felt. He didn't know a whole lot about what was going on, either, did he? But he knew more than she did, and he was willing to help. It occurred to her that perhaps she ought to feel grateful, though she hated to think about what he'd suspected her of doing.

Alyssa stepped forward, unsure if Chris was offering to take the baby or if he simply knew of some way to quiet the child. His arm curled around the baby's back, and his hand landed on her shoulder.

His touch had an immediate soothing effect on the baby, who'd turned his head the other direction and now seemed prepared to fall back to sleep. Alyssa froze half tucked into Chris's embrace, unwilling to move for fear of reawakening the baby. She'd had too much trouble getting him to calm down the last time and was in no state to figure out his cryptic baby ways if he started wailing again.

"Shh," Chris soothed, the sound hardly more than a breath. His face hovered just above the baby's, mere inches from hers. "Shh."

Alyssa wanted to believe he was making the sound for her nephew's benefit, but it had a soothing effect on her, as well. She drew in a long breath and felt her shoulders relax even as she detected the masculine scent of Chris's shampoo or aftershave, or whatever it was. She drew in another breath. The scent was faint but attractive.

She didn't want him to step away or let go of them. Everything felt out of control. She didn't think she could trust Chris, but nonetheless, it was comforting to stand there with him, with his strong arms hugging both her and the baby, like the family she'd lost too many times—first her parents, then her grandmother, her sister and finally her grandfather, until she was the only one left, as cold and unfeeling as the statues in her yard.

Chris's embrace made her feel human again, part of the world of people who lived and breathed, unlike the frozen concrete forms who made up her family most days.

"I believe you," he said in a tiny whisper, the words too faint to disturb the baby. "I believe someone has been planting drugs in your statues, but we need to catch them."

Still wary after the way he'd looked at her so accusingly not moments before, Alyssa wasn't sure if he meant the words or was only pretending to be on her side in order to get her to open up and tell him more.

She wanted him to believe her, wanted him to wrap his strong arms tighter around her and tell her everything was going to be okay. But everything had not been okay for the past eight years, so why should she allow herself to hope things would be different now?

Alyssa looked down at the downy-soft hair of the baby

she and Chris held between them, and she knew why she dared to hope. Because of this child, this baby she'd found in her manger. Because of him, she knew her sister was alive.

Looking up from the baby, she allowed herself to study Chris's face. He said he believed her. Looking into his eyes now, she believed him. Was he really on her side? She wanted him to be, wanted it so much it frightened her. Would it be crazy to trust him?

Maybe. But since she was truly innocent of any knowledge of the drugs, she figured she might as well tell him what she knew. Surely it would only help.

Too bad she didn't know much. "The little lambs are my bestselling items. It was an original design of mine—I cast the molds over a sculpture I made—I just figured people really liked it. But if they've been using them to smuggle drugs…well, I guess that explains why it sells so well."

"Do you have a record of who you've sold them to?"

"Not cash purchases, but I have the invoices for all the orders that came in from my website on my computer. But I can remember some of the local people who have bought a lot of the lamb statues with cash. I don't have records that prove they bought them, but if it would help just to know their names—"

"It would help," Chris insisted, still whispering quietly, still holding her and the baby. "Not everyone who bought the statues was necessarily smuggling drugs, but they're all worth looking into."

"Do you think so? I've had dozens of lamb statues stolen during the night before. Why would they buy them when they could just steal them?"

"Given the street value of those drugs, the cost of the statue is nothing to them. It was probably a question of which was easiest—buying during the day, stealing them at night. I suppose, once they realized you hadn't reported the crime, they figured stealing them was easier—no paper trail, no face to recognize from a cash sale. Maybe they thought they'd bought too many in person, and you might get suspicious."

"That makes sense," Alyssa admitted, mentally compiling a list of those who'd purchased the statues with cash over the past few years. "Dorothy Farris has bought several over the years, but she told me they were for her grandchildren."

"She doesn't strike me as the type who'd smuggle drugs," Chris admitted, "but you never can tell about people."

"Let's see, also Doug Larson, Marjorie Flint, Kathy Williams." She paused to sigh. "None of these people strike me as drug dealers." Then she laughed. "Oh, and Dick Edwards, the former police captain. I don't think any of them sound suspicious at all."

"Considering that they've probably been at it for years without getting caught, my guess is they're not going to be who you'd expect. They have a cover that works."

"You're probably right. I'll look over my shipping invoices and see if there are any repeat buyers."

"Do you have any record of when the other statues were stolen? Maybe we could find a pattern?"

"I noted the loss for tax purposes."

"I wish you'd filed a report."

Alyssa sighed. She couldn't go back in time and change her choice, but she could help Chris understand why she'd made it. "I didn't want to get the police involved. When my sister went missing, they seemed to think maybe I or my grandfather had done something to make her run away. They treated us like we'd done something wrong. And they never found her. So I didn't figure it would be worth the trouble to report anything."

Chris stayed silent, and Alyssa risked looking up from

her nephew's sleeping face to try to see what Chris was thinking. She hadn't realized his face was so close to hers. He looked angry.

"I'm sorry," she added, hoping to appease him.

"No, I'm sorry," he told her flatly. "I wasn't part of that area of the investigation, but I was on the force when your sister went missing. They shouldn't have treated you like that. There are a lot of things I would have done differently if I was in charge of the investigation, like grilling all the people who were at The Flaming Pheasant that night to see if they noticed anything out of the ordinary. They interviewed everyone, of course, but I wanted to go deeper, ask more questions—who had she been talking to, each day, every day before she disappeared? But when I brought it up, they told me not to—that I might throw off the investigation. I was new on the force and did what I was told, but in retrospect, I wish I'd trusted my gut."

Alyssa had done a good job holding back tears so far, but hearing his words and the regret in his voice, she felt her emotions getting the best of her. Rather than let him see, she took a step away, out of the warmth of his arms, and headed for the door from her studio to the main workshop.

She stepped through the doorway of her small art studio, around the chair, past the large shelving units that had blocked the main workshop from their view while they'd been in the studio, and froze. "Oh!"

Chris was one step behind her and clearly saw what she'd seen. "No." His voice fell. "No."

All the lamb molds that had been sitting on the counter, as well as the packet of heroin Chris had dug out and placed on the counter, were gone.

SEVEN

Chris sidestepped Alyssa on his way across the room, evaluating the empty countertop in a sweeping glance. Everything was gone except the mold he'd removed the heroin from. He turned to the door, which was still open, just as he'd left it when he'd burst in to make sure Alyssa and the baby were okay.

"I'm going to look outside."

"Are you sure it's safe? They had a gun."

Chris could have screamed with frustration. At the very least, he should have held on to the packet of heroin, but he hadn't wanted to touch it for fear of wiping out any residual fingerprints.

Now it was gone. In a flash, he realized his mistake. The guys had only just left when he arrived, but he hadn't seen any car lights. They hadn't ever really left, had they? They'd just ducked out and stuck around to watch what happened when Chris showed up moments later. And since Chris had left the door open, they'd had no trouble seeing everything. They'd probably watched him fish the drugs out of the mold, then waited and slipped in to grab it he and Alyssa were in the studio with the baby.

If he hadn't been so suspicious of Alyssa, so eager to see what was behind the little door, he'd have taken her claims about the intruders more seriously. But he hadn't trusted her until he'd stepped out of the room, turning his back on the evidence.

And since he wasn't on duty anymore, he wasn't wearing his body armor. He pulled the gun from his ankle holster, aware it was his only defense. Going outside would be dangerous.

But letting the smugglers run free wasn't an option.

"I'm just going to take a look around." He darted outside, gun up and ready. The darkness and the shadows made it difficult to see anything, but he knew one thing. Alyssa had said there were two guys. And five statues, complete with bulky molds, had gone missing. Besides being heavy concrete, they were close to two feet across in their longest direction. The smugglers wouldn't get far carrying them on foot.

They had to have a car somewhere. He ran for the road, looking up and down in both directions, gritting his teeth as he realized Alyssa lived in just enough of a valley that the hills on either side quickly blocked his view of the road.

They could have gone in any direction.

Or they could still be hiding out. The cluttered yard of concrete statues provided unlimited hiding places. Chris would have to walk up and down between all the statues in an attempt to find them—and in the dark, they could dart out of sight and hide elsewhere when he wasn't looking.

He pulled out his phone and called the police station, quickly relaying his location and the situation.

"Mitch is on patrol. I'll send him over."

Relieved to know he'd have an armed officer on his side in a few moments, Chris took another look around the yard. The smugglers could be anywhere nearby, waiting to eliminate Alyssa. If they realized she'd seen them, even in the dark, she could be in even bigger danger.

Chris ran back into the workshop, relieved when he saw Alyssa was okay, although the baby was crying again.

"Did I wake him up?" Chris realized he hadn't been very quiet at all. He'd been too upset that the evidence was missing.

"Do you think he wants another bottle?"

"It would probably help."

Chris escorted her back to the house, determined to check all the rooms to be sure no one was hiding inside. Fortunately, the cottage was tiny. There weren't many places anyone could hide. The fact only made him feel a tiny bit better.

Halfway through his search, the police cruiser arrived.

"What's that?" Alyssa looked up, startled, from preparing a bottle, as bright headlights pierced the windows.

"I called for reinforcements." Chris realized he should have mentioned the fact already, or perhaps even consulted Alyssa, since it was her property, but the baby was still crying, and it was difficult to talk. He ran outside to meet Mitch and let him know what they were looking for.

Then, while the officer performed a thorough search of the property, Chris went back inside. Alyssa had the bottle ready, and the baby quieted down to eat.

"I'm sorry I didn't tell you I was calling for backup. I just reacted. Two guys with guns—they outnumber us, and we don't know where they are."

"You did the right thing." Alyssa blinked rapidly as she looked down at her nephew, who was contentedly sucking the bottle. "I should have called when my statues went missing. Maybe we could have avoided all this."

"I understand why you didn't call." Chris cleared his throat. "I shouldn't have turned my back on the drugs we pulled from the statues. Now all the evidence is gone."

"If you hold the baby for me, I can pull up those files of orders. Maybe that will give us a clue."

Chris agreed readily. While Alyssa coaxed her aging computer to life, Chris stood, holding the baby and reading over her shoulder.

"I'll sort by item number," Alyssa explained once the order spreadsheet was open on the screen. Then she highlighted all the orders that contained the lamb and copied them to another page before printing off a couple of copies. "This way we can both look at it and underline orders from the same place."

Even before the pages emerged from the printer, Chris spotted several towns with multiple orders in Wisconsin. "Lake Geneva, Como, Delavan, Elkhorn. Can you open up a map of Wisconsin?"

Alyssa opened another tab and zoomed in on a cluster of lakes and golf courses hardly ten miles north of them, across the state line, in Wisconsin. All the little towns were within a mile or two of one another.

"I had vaguely realized I'd sent more than one order to this area," Alyssa admitted. "I just figured someone had seen my statues in a friend's yard and wanted one of their own. But obviously it wasn't my statue they were interested in. Still, they all shipped to different people, and the billing addresses match the shipping addresses. Do you really think there are that many different people involved?"

"Could be—but I doubt they'd want their names all over it. No, I'd say more than likely somebody just has a bunch of friends. All a guy would have to do is ask his golfing buddy to place an order for him, say it's a surprise gift and he doesn't want the wife to see it on the credit-card statement. He hands his friend cash, takes the statues and successfully dodges the paper trail." He'd recently heard about someone who'd moved up to Lake Geneva. While Chris explained the theory, he tried to remember. Who had it been? Before he could recall the name, Alyssa spoke.

"It makes me want to look up the people who ordered and ask them who the statues were for." She took the baby from him and leaned him against her shoulder again, burping him after his bottle.

"That might not be a bad idea. The only downside is, if they talk to the smuggler—or worse yet, if one of them is the smuggler—then you've tipped him off that you're on his trail. If he goes into hiding, we might never catch him."

Loud rapping echoed from the back door, and Mitch let himself inside. "The yard looks clear," his colleague announced. "No sign of anybody. Now explain about the missing heroin?" Mitch scratched the balding area where his hair used to be.

Chris filled him in on the drugs he'd found, including his suspicions about connections to the drug residue found on the statuary fragments in Pennsylvania. Mitch narrowed his eyes and looked concerned but didn't appear to be too surprised. Mitch wasn't surprised by much. He'd joined the force less than a year ago after working in law enforcement in Chicago and had mentioned before how much more laid-back life was in their small town.

As Chris wrapped up his explanation, showing Mitch the printed spreadsheets of Alyssa's order history, he remembered who'd moved to Lake Geneva. "You started on the force before Dick Edwards retired, didn't you, Mitch?"

"That's right."

"Doesn't he have a cabin in the Lake Geneva area?"

"Lots of folks do."

But now that he'd remembered, Chris was almost certain the recollection was correct. "Doesn't that seem like an odd coincidence?"

"Maybe. I need to get going. Can I talk to you alone for a moment?" Mitch headed toward the door.

Chris followed him out, glancing around the yard, wishing he could see something that would answer his many questions.

"Don't mess with Dick Edwards," Mitch told him bluntly once they were outside. "You don't want to get in over your head." The officer gave him a sharp look, then hopped into his patrol car and drove away.

The words churned uneasily in Chris's stomach as he went back inside and joined Alyssa.

She stood in the kitchen, the baby still fussing on her shoulder, though his cries weren't nearly so loud now, after the bottle. "He took my spreadsheets."

"Mitch took your spreadsheets?" Chris clarified, realizing then that he'd shown them to the officer, but hadn't intended to part with them. "As evidence?"

"I guess. But he didn't seem to think much of our theories."

Chris debated telling her what Mitch had said. He didn't want to worry her. But then, he got the sense she'd want to know. And maybe she'd have an insight into what was up.

"Mitch said something when we went outside. He told me not to mess with Dick Edwards—that I don't want to get in over my head."

"In over your head? Because he's a former captain?"

"He's retired now. He doesn't have any authority over me, other than maybe influence with the current captains and chief."

Alyssa continued to bob slowly up and down with the baby, who didn't seem happy, perhaps because he missed his mother. "How long has Edwards been retired?"

"Less than a year. Maybe six months."

"And these orders go back a few years." Alyssa looked at the last remaining spreadsheet. "How long has he had a cabin up there?"

"I didn't hear anything about it until his retirement, but that doesn't mean he hasn't had a vacation home up there, maybe even for years. What are you thinking?"

"Do you think maybe he knows about the statues and the drugs? Maybe he's trying to track them down, too."

Chris nodded slowly, analyzing the idea with the other facts he knew. "I first saw the story about the statues well over a year ago, before Edwards's retirement. He surely saw the same story. And you said he's bought statues from you? When was that?"

"I can't remember, exactly. They were cash purchases, so I don't have a record of the buyer's information, but it had to have been months ago, at least. Maybe a year or more. Do you think he bought them because he saw the story?"

"It's certainly possible." But Chris wasn't sure how to reconcile that information with what Mitch had said. "But why would Mitch tell me to stay away from him?"

Alyssa bobbed silently for a few more minutes, her expression puzzled, offering the baby his pacifier in an attempt to get him to settle down and fall back to sleep. She caught Chris off guard when she asked, "Is there a reward?"

"Hmm?"

"For catching the smugglers?"

"A pretty-good-size reward."

"Maybe Mitch is working with Dick Edwards."

Chris laughed at the thought. "Mitch and Edwards never got along. In fact, I was pretty relieved when Edwards retired, because those two had snapped at each other so many times, I was afraid they might take a swing at each other."

"Hmm." Alyssa rubbed her eyes with one hand, holding the baby with the other. "Maybe Mitch is working with the smugglers."

"What?"

"You said it had to be a good cover—that it would be someone we wouldn't expect."

But Chris was more concerned with the exhausted circles under Alyssa's eyes than he was with her theories, at this point. And more than either of those things, he was concerned for her ongoing safety. "You need your sleep. Why don't I take the baby while you go to bed? If you hurry, you might be able to get a few hours of sleep before morning."

Alyssa looked as if she wanted to protest, but when Chris reached for the baby, she handed him over, then rolled her head back. "I was getting a bad kink in my neck. That feels better. But I can't let you—"

"Go. Sleep. You'll be no good to anyone if you don't get some sleep."

"But what about you?"

"Is that chair a recliner?" He pointed to an aging afghan-covered seat in the corner.

"Yes."

"If the baby will let me sit still, I'll sleep in the recliner."

"I can sleep in the recliner with him. You can go home—"

"If I go anywhere, it will be out to my Jeep to watch over this place, but I'd rather be inside. The closer I am to you, the better I can protect you. The woods are too thick around here. Somebody could sneak up from any direction." Chris saw the fear that leaped to Alyssa's eyes and realized he'd made his explanation a bit too bluntly. "Not that they're going to, but I don't want to take any chances." He hung his head, wondering if he was making things better or worse. "You go get your sleep, okay?"

When Alyssa finally relented and shuffled off to her room, Chris watched her go. He stared at her closed door a few moments until the baby demanded his attention. Who was this woman who'd been making such art on the edge of town for so long, without his even realizing it? He'd been so worried about what illegal activities she might be engaged in that he hadn't ever really looked at *her*, hadn't ever really seen her.

Now that he'd met her and gotten to know her, he knew a few things for certain. He should have met her sooner. He should have been watching out for her, protecting her, instead of being suspicious of her. One way or another, he had to keep her safe. The smugglers had to be stopped, locked away where they could never bother Alyssa again.

And he knew one other thing.

He didn't want to go back to not having her in his life.

EIGHT

Alyssa awoke when the sun poured through her bedroom window, splashing across her face. The hazy remnants of dreams danced across her consciousness, taunting her. Broken statue. Guns. Drugs. Smugglers.

A baby. Vanessa was alive.

Throwing back the covers, Alyssa leaped up, put on her robe and tiptoed for the bathroom. She glanced into the tiny front room just long enough to see Chris asleep in the recliner, her grandmother's afghan spilled across his legs, the baby drooling all over his shirt. She lingered to watch their chests rise and fall, then she swallowed back a surge of foreign emotion and headed for the shower.

She emerged fifteen minutes later dressed and clean, ready to start her day. Other than waiting to put her hair in a ponytail, which she preferred not to do until her hair had some time to air-dry, she was ready to work. But first, she needed breakfast.

Having always had more time than money, she was used to doing most of her cooking from scratch. Besides, baking always brought back memories of her grandmother. And the freezer was full of blueberries from the bushes that grew behind the cottage. It didn't take long to stir together a batch of muffins.

When she pulled them from the oven, a movement in

the front room caught her eye. Chris had awakened but was still pinned to the recliner by her sleeping nephew. He waved one hand at her and mouthed, *Are those blueberry muffins?*

She nodded.

"Can you bring me one?"

"Do you want butter?"

He shook his head, and Alyssa brought him a muffin on a plate. "Careful, it's hot," she whispered. "Can I get you something to drink?"

"Milk?"

By the time she returned with the glass, he'd swallowed half the muffin. "These are real blueberries." He looked impressed. "Did you make this from scratch?"

She nodded. "It's a lot like mixing up cement."

"The muffins don't turn out as hard." He grinned at her.

Alyssa giggled, realizing only after a few moments that she was staring, perhaps a bit too obviously, at the handsome police officer. She directed her gaze to the baby instead and hoped Chris would think she'd been aiming the adoring look at her nephew the whole time. "Did he sleep all right?"

"Sure, once he finally filled his diaper. I think that was what was making him fussy."

"Oh. Sorry you had to deal with that."

"It comes with the territory. I personally think babies are worth the unpleasant side effects."

She would have been in danger of giggling and gazing a bit too long again except she had more urgent concerns on her mind. "I want to go to Wisconsin to Lake Geneva."

Chris nearly choked on a bite of muffin. "What?" He chewed quickly, his expression concerned. "When?"

"Today. As soon as possible." She explained while he washed down his mouthful of muffin with milk, "I figure I can either wait around to see if these guys are coming back, or I can do something about what's happening. If these smugglers have been using my statues for years, I don't want to wait—"

But Chris interrupted her. "It's dangerous."

"More dangerous than sitting quietly by while guys with guns hide their drugs in my statues?"

Chris's eyes narrowed. Alyssa thought for sure he was going to protest further, but instead he asked, "Can you be back by two?"

"I imagine so. Why?"

"That's when my shift starts. If you're determined to do this—"

"I *am* determined to do this."

"What are you looking for, anyway?"

"For one thing, I want my lamb molds back that the guys stole last night. They're an original design, but besides that, a lot of expensive materials went into those."

"Then I'm coming with you."

Alyssa had made a valiant effort to keep her surging emotions buried, but when Chris met her eyes with challenge and informed her he was coming, she felt gratitude and affection well up inside her. She knew she couldn't keep it from showing on her face. Nor could she trust her voice. Instead, she turned and hurried back to the kitchen.

After all, she hadn't had a muffin yet.

Chris watched Alyssa disappear in silence into the kitchen and wondered if he'd offended her. Even if he had, that wouldn't change his stance. If she was going anywhere near Lake Geneva, he was going to go with her. In fact, ever since he'd noticed the cluster of orders on her spreadsheet, he'd been curious to drive up there and check things out. He wasn't sure exactly what he was looking for or what he might find, but as Alyssa had pointed out, the smugglers had stolen her concrete molds. They had to be somewhere.

At the same time, though, he hoped he hadn't offended her. He wished he could go back in time and try again to make a better first impression on her. But since he couldn't, he figured the best thing he could do at this point was to keep her safe, to help her recover her stolen property and maybe even catch the smugglers.

And if he really wanted to earn her affection, he could help her find her sister, too. While it had always bothered him that the case had never been solved, now that there was evidence that Vanessa was still alive, he considered it unconscionable that they still hadn't found her. He owed it to Alyssa. He couldn't go back and change all the years the twins had been apart, but if he could help reunite them, maybe he wouldn't feel so guilty for not helping to solve the case years before.

More than that, maybe he wouldn't feel like such an imposter, helping out with the child when he'd failed to find the baby's mother. Other than those reservations, holding the child felt natural. It had been a long time since Chris had taken the night shift with a baby, at least since his youngest niece was old enough to sleep through the night. He missed the family scene.

Maybe it was time for a family of his own. The idea seemed to come from out of nowhere, and yet, it felt like the natural conclusion to reach while snuggled under an afghan with a sleeping baby. He couldn't help wondering what Alyssa's thoughts on the matter might be. But then, he was in no position to ask her. She'd stomped off to the kitchen in silence, and he couldn't help fearing that she was upset with him for insisting he accompany her to Wisconsin.

The baby awakened while Alyssa cleaned up in the

kitchen, and Chris eased himself out of the chair and joined her just as she finished hand-washing her muffin tins.

"Do you suppose he's hungry?" Alyssa asked. "Do you think it would be okay to feed him oatmeal again—at least until I can get to the store?"

"That should be okay. Do you mind if I use your computer while you make it?"

"Go right ahead."

Chris sat with the baby on his lap and searched for an address for Dick Edwards. Granted, he could have probably called around to his fellow officers until he found someone who had it, but he didn't want to tip off anyone to what he was up to. He already wondered if perhaps he shouldn't have said anything to Mitch earlier. The more he thought about it, the more he realized he didn't know much of anything about Mitch—and what he did know didn't help matters.

In fact, Alyssa's idea that Mitch might be working with the smugglers made all too much sense. He'd come to their tiny town from the big city, supposedly to get away from it all, but he didn't have any connections to the area. That alone made his choice suspicious. Factoring in his cryptic warning not to get involved with Dick and the way he'd carried off the spreadsheets, Chris didn't figure he ought to trust Mitch at all.

It didn't take him long to find Dick's Lake Geneva address, then to find it on a map amid clusters of other acreages and resort-style cabins. It looked like a pricey area, and Chris was a little surprised that the retired public servant had been able to afford a place in the exclusive region.

He added the location to the map he'd been compiling of the addresses from Alyssa's spreadsheet. He printed off the map and handed over the baby to Alyssa, who'd finished preparing a bottle and oatmeal.

"Mind if I take a look around outside now that it's daylight?"

"That's a great idea. Just be careful."

"I will." Chris stepped outside, still wondering at Alyssa's response to him. She didn't sound upset. She'd sounded grateful for his help and concerned for his safety. Was that a good sign?

He went outside and circled around to the woods behind the cottage. The narrow ravine with its stretch of trees didn't belong to Alyssa. Chris was pretty sure the property belonged to a man who kept a second home outside of town and used the wooded land for hunting. Only this tip of the ravine was inside the city limits. The rest stretched beyond into the country.

Chris crossed the ravine, headed for the gravel road just beyond the ridge on the other side. But as he looked for a decent place to clamber up the other side, he spotted something that looked familiar but terribly out of place.

One of Alyssa's lamb molds lay dented and muddy amid the underbrush. Drying cement spilled forth from it, but there wasn't any sign of the heroin inside. Chris carefully picked his way over, but didn't see any footprints as he approached. Scanning the area, he caught sight of a bunch of scrambling tracks etched into the side of the ravine about ten feet away.

So, the smugglers had fled on foot through the woods, run down the ravine and then realized the two of them couldn't carry five molds up the bank, so they'd fished the drugs from one and pitched it to the side, then clambered up and away.

Rather than risk messing up footprints that might be used as evidence, Chris headed back the other direction, found a decent place to climb up and then followed the top of the ridge back toward the spot where the smugglers had climbed out.

The road passed close to the woods, and Chris hurried over to inspect the tracks embedded in its surface. He didn't have to get close before he realized exactly what he was looking at.

Not only had Chris studied car tracks at the law-enforcement academy, but he'd also made it a point to note the distinctive traits of tread marks whenever he encountered them. Even if he hadn't, though, Chris would have had no trouble recognizing the tracks that topped the others on the rarely used gravel road. He saw the same tread marks every day in the alley behind the police station.

They belonged to the police cruisers.

Alyssa changed the baby's diaper and dressed him in a clean outfit before adding his clothes from the day before to the load of laundry she'd been planning to wash that day. Considering that she didn't have many clothes for him, she figured she ought to keep the ones she had fresh and clean.

Chris burst in the back door just as she came carried the baby up the basement steps from starting the load of wash. He panted slightly, as though he'd run all the way to her door from some distance.

"What's wrong?"

"I need to run by the station before we head out of town. Will that be okay?"

"No problem. What's up?"

Chris drew in a big breath. "I found one of your molds in the ravine. No drugs. Footprints go up the ravine toward the road. There are tire tracks that come to a stop near the footprints, then continue on down the road."

"Wow."

"There's more. The tracks belong to a police cruiser."

"Is that a good sign?"

"That road isn't inside the city. It's outside police jurisdiction. That doesn't mean an officer shouldn't be driving out there, just that he'd have no good reason."

"And you say the footprints—"

"I kept my distance because I didn't want to mess up any evidence, but yeah, the footprints lead right to where the car stopped."

"So, that Mitch guy from last night—"

"Could have stopped and picked up the smugglers." Chris filled in the words Alyssa had hesitated to speak. Then he explained, "That's why I want to swing by the station before we leave town. That road has a lot of yellow clay. The city streets are all paved. If the car Mitch drove last night has yellow clay on the tires, it will mean he most likely drove down that road and made the tracks."

"The baby and I are ready to leave whenever you are. Want us to come with you now? We can head to the police station first. It would be right on our way out of town."

"Sounds perfect. I just want to hurry before anybody drives the mud off the tires or, worse yet, washes the car. We can take my Jeep."

Alyssa appreciated the offer, since her old truck didn't do well on the highway. It sputtered and backfired at high speeds. She needed a new vehicle, but every time she saved up for a down payment, the money got eaten up by more urgent expenses.

They were halfway to the police station when the baby began to fuss, and Alyssa realized she'd left both pacifiers back at her house.

"Want me to turn around and go back for them?" Chris offered.

"He's not too fussy. We should check the tires as soon as possible. We can go back for the pacifiers before we leave town. We'll need them."

They pulled into the alley behind the police station, and Chris groaned.

"Yellow clay?" Alyssa identified, looking at the tires of the police cruiser parked in the small lot near the police station's rear entrance. "Is that the car—"

Chris nodded. "That's the exact car Mitch was driving when he came by last night."

"No wonder he was in such a hurry to leave."

"I just wish we hadn't shared so much. Now he knows everything we know, and he has the spreadsheet with the addresses."

"Do you think we should still head to Lake Geneva?"

Chris pulled away from the station and pointed the Jeep back toward Alyssa's place. "Mitch wouldn't have taken those addresses if they weren't important. We're just going to have to hurry—the morning is almost over, and I need to be back before my shift starts at two."

As they neared her home, Alyssa spotted a large SUV parked near her statuary lot. "Who do you suppose that is?"

"That looks like the same Sequoia that was driving off down the road yesterday when I responded to your initial call."

"You mean, when the baby—" Alyssa started to open her door even before the Jeep came to a stop. She couldn't see anyone, but if there was any chance her sister had dropped off the baby from the same vehicle—

"You need to be careful. That could be anyone."

But already one of the SUVs doors opened and a woman stepped out, turning her face so that the wind blew her blond hair back from her face. It was a face Alyssa hadn't seen in years, but which so closely resembled the one she saw in the mirror every morning.

NINE

"Vanessa!" Alyssa scrambled out of the Jeep and ran to her sister, wrapping her in her arms and squeezing her tighter than she'd ever squeezed anyone in her life. Then she pulled back just far enough to see into her sister's face, the face she feared she might never see again, to see that it was really her and to take in all the changes the past eight years had made.

It wasn't until Vanessa started sobbing that Alyssa realized she was crying, too—big tears flowing down her cheeks, dripping from her chin.

Then her sister looked past her for just a second and said, "Sammy looks happy. You did a good job with him. Was he too much trouble?"

"Sammy?" Alyssa looked behind her and saw that Chris had brought the baby carrier over. "You named him after Grandpa?"

Vanessa smiled at her sister knowingly. "I always said I would."

Alyssa hugged her sister again, amazed that, in spite of all the time that had passed between them and all the things she didn't yet know about her sister's time away, on some level, her sister was still the same girl she'd grown up with. It gave her hope that they could pick back up and put their family back together.

As she was hugging her sister, one of the SUV's doors opened, and a little girl peeked out. "Mommy? Is it time?"

"Yes, it's okay." Vanessa stepped back and held the door open as first one, then a second girl clambered out.

Alyssa felt the tears begin to flow again as she looked at little girls that reminded her so much of her and her sister at their ages. "You have two daughters?"

"This is Abby and Emma. Girls, this is your aunt, my twin sister I told you about."

"She *does* look just like you, Mommy. Just like you said."

The little girls tackled Alyssa in a hug, and she bent down to embrace them, amazed that she had nieces, that they knew about her, that they thought she looked just like their beautiful mother.

Chris cleared his throat behind them. "I think we should all go inside," he suggested.

Alyssa realized instantly the wisdom of his suggestion. "Let's *do* go inside." For all she knew, the smugglers might still be around. It was also a reminder that she and Chris had made plans to try to learn more about the smugglers in hopes of putting a stop to their crimes.

She wished the smugglers would wait so she could focus on her reunion with her sister and the nieces she hadn't known she had, but unfortunately, she'd observed enough of the criminals' work to know otherwise. If she let her guard down, they'd take advantage of her again.

The driver's door of the SUV popped open, and a man hopped out.

"You remember Eric Tomlin." Vanessa took the man's arm affectionately.

"I sold Grandpa's cabin to him."

"That's where she found me," Eric said.

"I fled to the cabin last night," Vanessa explained, "after

I dropped Sammy off with you. Eric was there. It was a little confusing at first, but then he helped me."

"Helped you what? Where have you been all these years?" Alyssa was as confused as ever. She held the front door open as everyone filed through.

Vanessa entered last, pausing to speak in hushed tones. "I have a lot to explain, but I don't want the girls to hear the details. I've protected them from the truth about our situation all these years. They have no idea what they've been through, and I don't want them to know, at least not until they're older and can understand it better."

"I still have all your dolls upstairs. The girls can go up to our old bedroom and play with them."

"You saved them!" Vanessa hugged her again. "That's perfect. Girls, come see the dolls I used to play with when I was your age."

Vanessa escorted the girls up the narrow stairs that led to what had once been a tiny attic, which their grandparents had converted into a bedroom for the twins when they'd come to live with them after their parents died. Alyssa hadn't used the room since her grandfather's health had declined following Vanessa's disappearance. He'd slept in the recliner because he had trouble getting out of bed, and she'd taken the downstairs bedroom so she could hear him when he needed help.

Then she'd stayed downstairs after he was gone, because the memories upstairs were more painful than the memories downstairs.

"Do you have a Bible here I could look at?" Eric asked.

"Sure. Let me grab it." Alyssa handed him the Bible from her nightstand as Vanessa came back down the stairs.

"So, where have you been? What happened?" Alyssa asked, unable to hold in her questions any longer.

"I was kidnapped by a human-trafficking ring and held

against my will. I was on the news last night—you didn't see any of it?"

"I had my hands full with the baby." Alyssa realized she hadn't so much as turned on the television at all in the past day.

Vanessa hurriedly explained, "My captor married me—he's the father of the kids. I won't get into the details now, because there's something more important. We caught the head of the human-trafficking ring this morning, but they were working closely with a drug-smuggling ring, and the people behind that are still at large. The authorities want me to go into hiding until they capture everyone behind the drug ring, too, because the two groups were working so closely together. I won't be safe until they've all been captured."

Alyssa felt her mouth drop open. "Drug trafficking. Like heroin?"

"Yes, exactly." Vanessa looked a little startled. "I think that was the main drug they traded."

Alyssa grabbed her sister's hand, looking straight into her eyes as she had so many times when they were young. "What ever happened to your keys?"

"My keys?"

"Yes—your keys to this house, the workshop—"

"The kidnappers took them."

Alyssa let out a long breath and looked at Chris. "Do you think they could be related?"

"It's certainly possible. In fact, it might explain why someone would work so hard to frame you—to build up a cover story, to frame your sister if she ever escaped." He addressed Vanessa. "Who were these people? What are their names?"

"Arthur Sherman was the man behind everything."

"The owner of The Flaming Pheasant?"

Vanessa nodded. "It was one of their cover operations

for the businesses that really made them money—drugs
and human trafficking. But Arthur was only in charge of
the human trafficking, as far as I understand it. Someone
else was in charge of the drug ring. But what are you two
talking about—is *what* related?"

Alyssa hated to frighten her sister more after all she'd
been through, but she hoped perhaps by sharing information, they might be able to sort out what was going on.
"Drug smugglers have been using my sculptures to hide
their drugs. They broke into my workshop again just last
night."

"That's it!" Vanessa gasped. "I overheard them last
night. One of Arthur's guys was talking about keeping
surveillance on you. He said somebody was going to run
a job."

"Somebody?" Chris asked. "Who?"

"They said a name. They said they were going to run a
job, whatever that means. Drug smuggling? What was the
name? It was a man's name. A plain, middle-aged-sounding
name. I was so terrified when I heard them say they were
watching you, I wasn't thinking about the name. I was trying to sort out what it meant."

"It's okay." Alyssa was too happy about seeing her sister
again to let that small detail upset her happiness. "Maybe
you'll think of it."

"Maybe I will. But whoever it is, the authorities hope they
can catch them quickly. Now that the human-trafficking ring
has been busted, they're afraid the drug smugglers will go
into hiding, and it will be that much more difficult to find
them if they can't catch them now."

"So, the local smugglers and the drug smugglers as-
sociated with the trafficking ring are one and the same.
It's too much of a coincidence otherwise." Chris crossed
his arms over his chest, his expression determined. "I'm
going to head up to Wisconsin right now. If these guys are

about to go into hiding, I want to learn what I can before the trail dries up."

Alyssa suddenly realized that, for all her concern, wanting to catch the drug smugglers, she'd rather spend time with her sister. They had so much catching up to do—she couldn't bear the thought of being separated from her so soon. "I think I might stay with Vanessa."

But Vanessa shook her head. "You can't."

"What? Why not?"

"The authorities are waiting at the top of the hill. I'm supposed to go into hiding. They said they'd give me half an hour to pick up Sammy, but no longer. They don't want to risk losing me. I'm a witness. I've probably stayed here too long already. I need to go."

"It's been twenty-five minutes." Eric had been paging through Alyssa's Bible and now held it open. "Mind if I take a minute to read this to you guys? When I was waiting on the hillside, just before Arthur Sherman ran toward me and I captured him, a sparrow landed near me and reminded me of this verse. But it wasn't until I found it just now that I realized how appropriate it is."

"Please read it." Chris sounded interested.

"From Matthew, chapter ten. 'Do not fear them which kill the body, but are not able to kill the soul. Are not two sparrows sold for a farthing? Not one of them shall fall. Fear not therefore, you are of more value than many sparrows.'"

Alyssa felt her throat tighten at the encouraging words. She didn't want to be parted from her sister, but if the authorities wanted Vanessa to go into hiding, she wasn't going to argue with them. And perhaps the best thing she could do was to look into the lead with the drug smugglers. If they could catch everyone involved, then Vanessa could come home to stay. "Thank you. I needed to hear that." She hugged her sister and her nieces, exchanged phone numbers and watched them leave with Eric, reassured by the words he'd read from the Bible. When the SUV reached the top of the hill, an unmarked vehicle pulled out and followed them out of sight.

When they were gone, Alyssa turned to Chris, feeling empty now with no baby to hold and her sister gone again. "I'm going with you. Remember, it was my idea."

"We need to get moving. My shift starts in three hours. And every minute we waste is another minute the smugglers have to go deeper into hiding." He led the way to his Jeep, and they both hopped in.

"What's your plan?" Alyssa asked as they headed north toward Wisconsin.

"I'm going to check out those addresses of the folks who ordered your lambs. And I might swing by Dick Edwards's place. Maybe he can help answer my questions. If he knows something, even if it's not enough to bring these guys in, maybe it will help tip the scales with the rest of the clues we've put together. At the very least, maybe we'll learn something before these guys destroy the evidence."

Alyssa watched him fiddle with a pair of handcuffs in his center console. "Are you going to try to arrest them?"

"I don't have any authority over there because it's outside of my jurisdiction, but if I see anything, especially if it looks like these guys are going somewhere, I've got the number for the Drug Enforcement Agency on my phone. They're not bound by state lines."

Chris drove as quickly as he legally could, his thoughts swirling in a whirlpool of adrenaline. He had to hurry to catch the guys who'd done so much to hurt Alyssa and her sister. He was thrilled that Vanessa was back—completely astounded, really. But at the same time, it only reinforced his failure as a police officer. Because Vanessa had been out there the whole time, but he hadn't been able to find her.

And with her return, Chris had lost all hope of earning Alyssa's affection by finding her sister. He felt that much worse that she hadn't reported her stolen statues because she didn't believe the local police could actually help her. She'd even feared them on some level.

It burned inside him. He *had* to catch the drug smugglers—to show Alyssa he cared, that he was a competent officer who could be trusted. That he could protect her. And because the criminals had flaunted their ability to break the law far too long.

But at the same time another thought buzzed in his head, frustrating him. He'd seen Arthur Sherman before, a long time ago. The memories were faint, buried by time, but he dredged them up as he drove northward, remembering.

He'd gone to The Flaming Pheasant a couple of times in the wake of Vanessa's disappearance. The captain in charge of the investigation had told him not to ask questions of Vanessa's fellow employees. So he'd kept his mouth shut, ordered a meal like any other customer and gone quietly on his way. He'd gone hoping for answers, because he hadn't been able to stay completely away, but he'd never learned anything.

But that was where he'd seen Arthur Sherman—not in real life, but in a picture on the wall, along with a couple of paragraphs welcoming customers to his restaurant. Where else had he seen him since then?

Before he could remember, he came up a road that led toward the first house of the many in the immediate area that had ordered little lamb statues from Alyssa. She found the house on the map for him, and he slowed down as they approached. Both of them scoured the yard for any sign of a lamb statue.

"There's a bunny statue under the tree," Alyssa identified as they drew closer. "That's one of my designs."

"Maybe when they went on the website to order the lamb, they saw the bunny statue and decided to buy it, too."

"That makes sense," Alyssa conceded, "but where's the lamb statue? Those two are of relative size. It would make sense for them to be placed together."

"Unless they bought the lamb for their friend and the bunny for themselves."

"And broke open the lamb for the drugs," Alyssa finished glumly. "So far, your theory holds."

Chris felt only the slightest reassurance from that fact. "Let's check out the next house on the list. It's not far."

The second house had no sign of any concrete statues in the yard, just a few bushes and the autumn remnants of a flower bed in a neat, landscaped arrangement.

"The next house is Dick Edwards's," Alyssa noted, studying the map. "The others are mostly on the other side of him. He's located almost in the middle of their circle—that fits your theory, if he moved here intentionally to try to catch the smugglers."

"Let's drive by and see if there's anything to see." Chris took the turn that led them into a neighborhood of small acreages, sweeping lawns neatly mowed, with tennis courts and tiny ponds fed by fountains.

"Nice neighborhood," Alyssa observed.

"Looks like somebody doesn't like it here, though. They're moving out." Chris pointed to a driveway up ahead, where two moving vans sat in the wide driveway, men traveling back and forth like drone bees, carrying boxes into the vans.

"That's Dick's house." Alyssa looked at the map, then back to the house again, repeating the address from Chris's notes even as his eyes confirmed the number on the mailbox.

"Why is Dick moving out?" Chris wondered.

"I thought the smugglers were the ones who were supposed to be going into hiding. Unless—" She gasped. "My sister said it was a male name, a common, middle-aged male name. Dick, maybe? I'm going to call her."

Chris drove past the house and turned at the next corner.

"Where are you headed now?"

"The back side."

"There isn't a back side." Alyssa gestured to the map with one hand while she held the phone with the other. "There's just woods and a field—there's not another road for half a mile."

But Chris's thoughts were flying, the pieces falling into place quickly now. "That's where I saw Arthur Sherman— at Dick's house back home, before he retired. I stopped by to bring him some paperwork that needed his signature. Sherman was there. They seemed—chummy."

"The police captain? You don't think he was investigating—" She turned her attention suddenly to the phone conversation. "Yes, Eric? Can I talk to my sister?"

"No, I don't think he was investigating," Chris answered her unfinished question in a whisper, gripped the steering wheel tightly, wishing he'd seen past Dick's veneer sooner.

Alyssa posed the question to her sister. An instant later, she ended the call to tell him what he'd already gathered from her side of the conversation. "Yes, that was the name of the drug smuggler. Dick. She didn't hear a last name, but it fits with everything else."

"It fits," Chris admitted, regretting he'd never doubted his former superior officer before. "We trusted him be- cause of his position, but he was using that position to stay ahead of the law, wasn't he? That's why he didn't want us asking questions at The Flaming Pheasant—because he's smuggling drugs and working with kidnappers."

TEN

Alyssa wanted to scream. "The police captain has been smuggling drugs out of my garage with my sister's keys, which he stole from her after his buddies kidnapped her?"

"That's what it looks like to me."

"I'm going to throw up. What a low-life dirty crook!"

"I concur. But we're going to catch him." Chris had taken the next road that ran parallel to the back side of Dick's property and now pulled to a stop half a mile from Dick's house, well hidden by the woods. He turned off the Jeep and pulled out his phone. "I'm calling the DEA."

Alyssa sat, fuming, wishing she could capture Dick Edwards that very moment, hoping the agents would hurry, and yet, at the same time, terrified because they'd driven past the smuggling kingpin's house. What if one of the men recognized Chris's Jeep? What if they came after them?

Chris ended the call after relaying all the vital information. "They're sending a team out, but it could take a while for them to arrive. We're in a remote location."

"So, now what do we do? Those guys are moving out. If they leave before the DEA agents get here—"

"I know." Chris opened his door. "We can't let them do that."

"Where are you going?" Alyssa jumped out and met him behind the Jeep, where he was rummaging in a duffel bag in the back end.

"Can you hold these?" He handed her a pair of binoculars from the bag, then made a face. "I don't have my camera. I'll have to use the one on my phone. I just hope the zoom is good enough." He pulled out a small notepad and a pen.

"You're going to spy on them and take pictures? Isn't that dangerous?"

"If they leave before the DEA agents get here, we'll need to gather as much intel as we can now. That means pictures of faces, if I can get a clear shot. License plates. Identifying marks. Evidence we can use to get a warrant later." He reached for the binoculars and paused as his fingers clasped hers. "You may want to stay with the Jeep."

"What would that accomplish? It's not like I could drive through the woods to pick you up if they spotted you—the trees are too thick."

"I just want you to be safe." He met her eyes.

For a moment, she couldn't breathe. The way he said the words, the concern on his face—no, it was more than concern. Or did she simply want it to be more than concern?

"I won't be safe until these guys are behind bars. Let's go." She held the notepad and pen, while Chris carried his phone and the binoculars.

They hiked quickly through the woods, pausing now and then for Chris to focus the binoculars in the direction of Dick's house. As they drew nearer, their pace slowed and they paused more often.

He focused the field glasses for a long moment. "I can see the license-plate numbers. Write these down."

Alyssa wrote as Chris told her the letters and numbers. She was so focused on getting the combinations correct, she didn't notice the vehicle approaching on the road they'd left behind them until she heard the distinctive sound of a car door closing.

"Who's that?" she asked, glancing backward, where a red car had come to a stop near Chris's Jeep. A couple of guys got out and headed for the woods.

"That looks like Mitch's car." Chris lifted the binoculars to his eyes again. "It's Mitch and some other guy I don't recognize." He tugged on Alyssa's sleeve. "Get down."

Already afraid that they may have been seen driving past Dick's house, Alyssa put the pieces together. "Mitch is working with Dick?"

"Of course." Chris shook his head regretfully. "He'll recognize my Jeep for sure. He knows we're out here."

Alyssa glanced around frantically. While too thick to drive through, the woods didn't offer sufficient cover to hide them if they tried to run away. Most of the trees were narrower than her hips—not promising cover to hide behind. And the bushes had lost their leaves for the fall. "Where are we going to hide? We can't run toward Dick's house—there are more guys there than here."

"We'll have to make a run for the Jeep now that the guys have left their car and are looking for us in the woods."

"They'll see us for sure, then." As it was, she figured it was only a matter of time before Mitch and his buddy got close enough to see them. But what other choice did they have?

"There's enough of a ridge between us. If we run along this side of the ridge, parallel to the road, and then turn back to the Jeep, we may be able to get to the vehicle ahead of them." Chris pulled his face closer to hers as he spoke, dropping his voice to a hollow whisper.

"Unless they have a gun."

Defeat crossed his face. "Fine, then. We both run. If they spot us or shoot, you run for the Jeep and I'll try to divert their attention." He pressed his keys into her hands.

She refused to take them. "There's no way I'm leaving without you." Still, she tore the page with the license numbers from the notepad and began to copy the digits onto the next page to give to Chris. Not knowing what might happen, she wanted the important information in as many hands as possible.

Distantly, the sounds of shoes crunching through leaves and undergrowth reached them through the woods. The men were searching for them, no doubt about it, but with half a mile or so of woods, they had a lot of ground to cover before they reached them.

"Don't be afraid. You are worth more than many sparrows," Chris whispered beside her.

"Hmm?" Alyssa finished jotting down the numbers and looked up to see a pair of sparrows sitting on a branch nearby. "Do you think God is trying to tell us something?"

"I think God is watching over us, always."

Something in the reassuring tenor of his words or the way he spoke them, his bluish-gray eyes focused on her face, sent a foreign shiver down Alyssa's spine. It wasn't a frightened shiver at all, but a warm, reassuring feeling of being cared for. God cared enough to send a pair of sparrows to reassure her. And Chris cared—how much, she didn't know, but he'd made too many sacrifices on her behalf for her to believe he was simply doing his job.

She held out the paper she'd copied. "Does that mean everything will be okay?"

"I don't know." Chris reached for the paper and wrapped his fingers around her hand. "I know He brought your sister back—and I didn't think we'd ever see her again. I think God keeps working even when we've given up hope. He is more faithful."

"He is more faithful." Alyssa repeated the words in a whisper as the sounds of the men crashing through the woods drew progressively closer. She drew in a full, steadying breath, grateful for the sparrows and her sister's return. But God hadn't just sent the birds—God had sent Chris into her life, hadn't He? The timing had been perfect. She wouldn't have known how to handle her nephew without Chris's help.

And she enjoyed his company, too. Even now, in the woods, with dangerous men stomping toward them, she felt an uncanny sense of peace just knowing Chris was with her. God had sent him to protect her, too. She was sure of it. And just as surely, she knew she'd miss him when he was no longer by her side.

Chris rose up slightly on his heels and glanced in the direction of the sounds. "They're moving away from us, searching in that direction," he whispered, his hand still holding hers.

"Should we run?"

"At my signal." He shoved the paper into his pocket.

Alyssa could hear the sound of the men approaching, but she couldn't see anything from where she and Chris crouched, and she didn't want to stick her head up for fear of giving away their location. Still, it sounded as though the distance between them and their pursuers was as broad as it might get. She mouthed the words in a near-silent whisper, *Should we run now?*

This is our best chance, Chris mouthed back. *Stay low.*

He kept hold of her arm for the first couple of steps, then let go as his pace increased.

Alyssa ran alongside him, her attention focused on the uneven, leaf-covered forest floor as she tried to plant each step strategically to avoid making noise or slipping and falling.

Behind her, she could hear crashing noises as Mitch and his buddy took off after them, heedless of the noise they made.

They'd been spotted!

Chris glanced back. Mitch and the other dude were way too close already, easily within accurate shooting range, even if he and Alyssa were moving targets. If it had only been Mitch behind him, Chris might have tried to fight him, but as it was, he was outnumbered, and he couldn't stand the thought of Alyssa getting hurt.

"This way!" Abandoning the ridge, he leaped downhill, changing direction, intent on reaching the Jeep. He'd stayed tight by Alyssa's side, but now, his goal the driver's door on the far side of the vehicle, he sped up ahead of her, intent on reaching it in time to have the engine started and the Jeep in Reverse by the time she jumped inside.

The sounds of pursuit crashed behind him, but thankfully, he hadn't heard any gunshots yet. Then a softer crash sounded far too close, and Chris looked back to see Alyssa flattened on the ground.

Had she tripped?

Or were the men shooting, using a silencer?

Chris leaped back to her side just as she lifted herself up. "You okay?"

"I'm fine. Run!" Alyssa regained her feet, but already the men, who'd been so close at their heels before she fell, were upon them.

One grabbed Alyssa's arms. "Run!" she shouted again.

Chris saw the fear on her face, understood what she meant. She wanted him to run to safety, to turn in the license-plate numbers and tell what he knew. To do whatever he could, if he could, to catch the bad guys. He needed to do all that.

But he couldn't turn his back and leave without her.

In that moment's hesitation, Mitch leaped around his partner and tackled Chris, holding him roughly with both arms behind his back. "What are you doing out here?"

Chris clamped his mouth shut, thinking quickly. Maybe he could talk his way out of trouble. Maybe there was still a chance.

But Alyssa glared at their captors furiously. "We already called the DEA," she growled. "They'll be here any minute. If you want to save yourselves, you better run now."

Chris might have smiled at her bravado had their circumstances not been life-threatening.

"The DEA, huh?" Mitch sneered. "Who'd you talk to?"

Unsure why Mitch would ask, but nonetheless feeling

compelled to back up Alyssa's story—which was buying them time for the DEA agents to arrive, if nothing else—he shared the name of the person he'd spoken to on the phone.

"I'll see about that." Mitch pulled out his phone and dialed.

Chris listened to the one-sided conversation, mystified. He initially assumed Mitch was calling the guys at the house, telling them to abandon whatever was left and make a run for it. But nothing Mitch said matched that scenario. Instead, his side of the conversation made it sound as though he was actually talking to the same person in the DEA office that Chris had spoken to, confirming the story.

"Yup, that's all. Tell them to hurry. Thanks." Mitch ended the call and looked at Chris with narrowed eyes. "What made you think it was a good idea to move in on armed drug smugglers? You're way outside of your jurisdiction."

Chris might have reminded Mitch that he was, too… only now he wasn't so sure. "Let me see your badge."

Mitch held it out—not his police badge, but a very official-looking badge that indicated he worked for the DEA. The guy who was with Mitch showed his badge, as well.

"Undercover?" Chris asked Mitch, though the answer seemed obvious now.

"We knew Dick Edwards was involved with the drugs. We just didn't know how. Now that his human-trafficking associates have been captured, we have enough witnesses to bring him in. My guys will be here shortly. I need you to get out of the way."

Chris let out a relieved breath. Mitch wasn't working for the smugglers—he was actually a DEA agent who'd been working undercover, investigating. That explained his mysterious arrival from the city, the tension between him and Dick—it explained everything.

He and Alyssa were going to be okay? It was almost too much to accept so quickly, no matter how glad he was about the news. But Mitch's badge was real, no doubt about it, so Chris dipped his head in acknowledgment. "We'll do that." Then he glanced at the road, quickly considering his options. "Which way do you want us to go?"

Mitch looked up and down the road in both directions and scowled. "Head down the road that way. Don't come around this way—you'll have to go around the lake and north. I don't want you anywhere near my men. This could get messy."

Chris agreed and took Alyssa's hand to help her back to the Jeep, leaving Mitch and his fellow officer behind. "Are you okay? That was quite a tumble."

"I tripped on a branch. My ankle isn't too happy about it, but I don't think it's sprained or anything—just wrenched. You should have kept running."

They reached the Jeep, and Chris opened the passenger-side door for Alyssa. "Run away and leave you?"

"Run away with the license numbers so the authorities could catch those guys. If Mitch really had been working for the smugglers, he'd have us both right now."

"I couldn't leave you." Chris moved his hand from the Jeep door to Alyssa's shoulder.

She didn't shrink away at his touch but looked at him in wonderment, the anger fading from her eyes. "That was a really stupid thing to do," she chided him, her voice soft. A smile tugged at the corner of her mouth, but she fought it back. "I just hope they catch all those guys so my sister can come out of hiding."

At that reminder, Chris remembered that, though the two of them may have gotten away from Mitch, nonetheless, they were still in dangerous territory. "We should head down the road."

Chris climbed into the Jeep and drove slowly, in silence,

wondering where everything stood. He wanted the DEA guys to catch all the smugglers, but at the same time, if the smugglers were out of the picture, Alyssa wouldn't need him around anymore. She didn't even need his help with the baby because her sister had returned.

Her life was full now, fuller than it had been in years.

And he couldn't recall when he'd felt so acutely alone. He wanted to be part of Alyssa's life, but he'd known her such a short time. If the smugglers were all captured, would he ever see her again?

Alyssa sat with her ankle in the most comfortable position and tried to catch her breath. She could have kicked herself for the words she'd said. But frankly, she hadn't known how to respond when Chris said he couldn't leave her behind. He'd risked his life to stay by her side. True, it had been a stupid move on his part, but it was also incredibly chivalrous.

She couldn't leave things the way she had. He'd done too much for her. "Chris, can you stop a second?"

The Jeep slowed immediately.

"Oh, I didn't mean literally." Alyssa started to apologize but then decided she had to plow ahead with what she needed to say if she was going to have the confidence to say it. "I just wanted to tell you, that was actually really cool what you did back there, coming back for me. I mean, it could have ended badly, but you did it, anyway. And helping me with the baby and everything. I don't know what I would have done without you."

The Jeep rolled to a stop, and Chris turned to face her, his dimple winking at her from his cheek as he spoke. "I enjoyed getting to know you. I'm glad I was able to help."

Alyssa looked into his eyes for a long moment, a giddy happiness rising inside her. Then, self-consciously, she looked past him out the window. Her mouth fell open.

"You can see everything from here. They're here. They're moving in!" She realized she'd interrupted Chris at a terrible moment, but there was nothing else for it. They'd driven past the woods to a place where an open field rolled between hills, giving them a perfect view of the house and the battle that was going on in the driveway and yard. Agents tackled smugglers, subduing them on the ground and cuffing their hands behind their backs.

"Oh, wow. There were a lot of them, weren't there? I had no idea." She watched, fascinated by all that was unfolding little more than a mile away. "Uh-oh. One of them is getting away."

"I see him." Chris raised his field glasses and zeroed in on the man who'd burst from the patio doors of the walkout basement, riding a four-wheeler. For a moment, he seemed to go unnoticed by the agents. One tried to chase after him on foot but was quickly outdistanced. Two others ran for their vehicles, but the cars were parked on the front side of the house. They'd have to go around by way of the road. It would take them a while to catch up— assuming they were even able to follow the ATV before it sped out of sight.

"He's going to get away!" Alyssa realized aloud.

Chris made a face into his binoculars. "It's Edwards."

"Dick Edwards?"

"Yes." Chris set the binoculars back in the console and put the Jeep in gear.

ELEVEN

Alyssa held on to the door handle as the Jeep churned across the ditch and chugged into the open field, picking up speed. She glanced toward the house and saw that a couple of DEA cars had taken off down the road, presumably to come around after Edwards. But he'd gotten too much of a head start. They'd have to go around the long way on the road—she doubted the vehicles could handle the uneven off-road terrain.

Fortunately, Chris's Jeep was accelerating quickly in spite of the rugged field. Chris set a course to bisect Edwards's path.

They were close enough now that Alyssa could see the former police captain clearly. He reached inside his jacket and pulled something out. "Careful! He's got a gun."

"He's going to have trouble firing *and* outrunning us," Chris predicted. Nonetheless, he adjusted his course so they were slightly behind the ATV, which was headed for the smooth road ahead. Even from that position, they continued to gain on the escaping criminal.

Knowing Edwards would be in a better position to fire the gun once he reached the level surface of the road, Alyssa looked around frantically for something to use against him. There were handcuffs in the center console, but those wouldn't be much use yet. She looked in the backseat and spotted a couple of cans of tennis balls next to Chris's racket.

Grabbing the cans, she rolled down her window. Ahead of them, Edwards rocketed the ATV up the ditch and onto the road. The Jeep lurched as it followed the same path.

"Careful!" Chris warned her as Alyssa leaned out the window. "He's going to try to use the gun now that he's on the road."

Alyssa understood the risk she was taking, but she couldn't let the former police captain get away. Not only had he been working with the kidnappers who'd taken her sister, but he'd also deliberately hindered the search efforts to find her. And if he got away, Vanessa and her children would never be able to come out of hiding.

No, Alyssa had no intention of letting the crook get away or even shoot out their tires. She popped open a can of tennis balls, dumped the first ball into her hand and swung. The ball flew past Edward's head, startling him. For an instant, the ATV slowed, but then surged forward again.

"He's right-handed," Chris informed her as the Jeep accelerated. "I'm going to try to come up on his left side. As long as I keep you behind him, he won't be able to hit you."

"Good plan," Alyssa agreed. She saw one of the DEA cars coming up behind them, over a mile away, having had to drive around via the road to reach them. She prayed the car would catch up quickly.

Dumping another ball into her hand, she waited a moment for Chris to pull up closer to the ATV and then took aim.

The ball glanced off Edwards's shoulder. He glared back at them. But, as Chris had predicted, he couldn't get a shot off as long as they stayed on his left side.

She dumped the last ball from the can into her hand and aimed for Edwards's right arm—the hand that held the gun.

The ball just missed.

At the same time, she saw the second DEA car pull onto the road less than a mile ahead of them. Hope rose inside her. They were going to cut him off!

But Edwards clearly saw the car, as well. He swerved madly as he turned his head, looking this way and that for an escape route. Thick woods on his right. The sprawling construction site of an expanding subdivision on his left.

He went left.

Chris followed.

Alyssa opened the second can of tennis balls.

Just ahead of them, Edwards swerved to avoid the excavated pit of what might soon be a basement or swimming pool. Chris took the tight corner, coming up on Edwards's right side.

Knowing this might be her best chance to knock the gun from the criminal's hand while he was too distracted to shoot, Alyssa let fly a well-aimed ball. It flew past the man's knuckles.

She grabbed another ball as the ATV swerved onto a paved street.

The Jeep accelerated as Chris stayed on the criminal's trail.

Alyssa glanced back. She could only see one DEA vehicle now. It had turned back to reach a road that would bisect Edwards's path—assuming Edwards continued on in the same direction. But with every change of course, the fugitive came closer to effectively evading the agents who'd arrested so many of his associates. Alyssa couldn't stand the thought that he might get away.

She had two balls left. She needed to make them count. "Can you get me closer?"

Chris gunned the engine. "We've got to stop him soon—there's a shopping district up ahead. I'd hate to lose him in the crowds."

Alyssa could see the cluster of stores a mile or two

ahead of them. She hated to think of Edwards using his gun among so many people. Innocent people could be injured or killed—and from what she knew of Edwards, he wouldn't let the risk of that stop him. He'd probably use it to his advantage.

As Chris pulled even with the ATV, close enough for her to see the gun clearly, she threw one ball and then the other, smacking Edwards roughly on the forearm both times.

But both times, he clung to the gun.

Alyssa glanced back. She couldn't see any sign of the DEA vehicles, but they were within half a mile of the first sprawling parking lot, crowded with vehicles, shopping carts and people.

She couldn't let Edwards get away. There was only one other thing she could think to do. As Chris steered the Jeep into the ATV, bumping tires, trying to shove the four-wheeler from the road, Alyssa pulled herself free of the window, swung one leg out, pulled the other foot onto the door's armrest and then planted one shoe onto the seat behind Edwards's back.

Chris must have realized what she was doing. He kept the Jeep tight with the vehicle as Alyssa pushed free of the window, landing hard on Edwards's back, punching madly against his right arm with all her strength, little caring if they crashed or what happened.

Because of this man, she hadn't seen her sister for the past eight years. No way was she going to let him get away.

Hooking one leg around the man's back, she got her right leg free and kicked his arm—hard. The gun dropped onto the concrete with a clatter, quickly falling behind as the ATV careened forward, out of control now as Edwards tried to fight her off his back. She ground her foot into his hand, as much to keep her balance as anything, though it had the added effect of disabling his grip on the throttle.

The ATV slowed to a stop.

Chris stopped the Jeep beside her, leaped out with the handcuffs in one fist, ran around the front of the vehicle and jumped on Edwards.

"Jensen? You're way out of your jurisdiction!" Edwards yelled at him. They struggled for a few moments, but Chris was clearly the stronger of the two.

Chris slapped a cuff on Edwards's right wrist and wrestled him against the seat of the ATV while Alyssa helped hold him down. Cuffing the other wrist, he pulled him upright and turned him to face the approaching DEA vehicle. "They've got jurisdiction," Chris said as he shoved him toward the approaching agent.

Alyssa slid down, panting from effort and relief. She heard Chris talking to the DEA agent, but she didn't look up, simply stared at her trembling hands in wonder. Had she really dived out the open window of the Jeep to subdue the former police captain? More important, would her sister now be free to come home?

Chris made sure the agent could handle the former police captain, before he turned his attention to Alyssa. She had her head down and appeared to be shaking. Probably shock from all that had happened. He could hardly believe she'd jumped out the window—but he doubted they could have caught Edwards if she hadn't.

He ran to her side and placed a hand on her shoulder. When she looked up at him with moisture pooled in her eyes, he pulled her into his arms. She held him tight, burying her face against his shoulder.

"Is it over?"

"I spoke to the DEA agent. He said everyone else at the house was captured."

"So, Vanessa can come out of hiding?"

"I think so." He didn't want to raise Alyssa's hopes too

much, but from what he could tell, everyone had indeed been arrested. "Everything is going to be okay."

"Is it? I gave up hoping a long time ago."

"I'm sorry I didn't find your sister for you," Chris confessed.

"But she's back." Alyssa looked confused.

"I know she's back now—but I mean we should have found her eight years ago. If I'd followed my instinct and pushed to interview The Flaming Pheasant employees, instead of following Edwards's orders—"

Alyssa cut him off. "He was your boss. Chris. It's not your fault she was gone for eight years. You did more to bring her back than anyone I know. If we hadn't caught Edwards just now, if he'd gotten away, she'd still have to be in hiding. She can come home now because of you."

Chris held Alyssa tight as the truth of her words sank in.

"Thank you." She pulled away from his embrace and looked into his eyes. "Thank you for everything you did. Thank you for driving like a madman across fields and a construction site—"

"It was kind of fun," Chris admitted with a chuckle.

The distress fled from Alyssa's face, and she managed a smile. "It was a little fun, wasn't it? I mean, now that it's over and no one got hurt." She looked up and noticed movement near the Jeep. "A sparrow."

The little bird hopped along the Jeep's bumper, looked at them a moment and then flew away. The bird reminded her of the Bible verse Eric had read. But more than that, it reminded her that they had places to go. She looked back toward the DEA car, where the agent had placed Edwards in the backseat and was ready to drive away. "Do you think it's okay for us to head home? I want to see my sister, and your shift starts in less than an hour."

"Let me clear it with the agents. Then we can go."

Chris made sure the Drug Enforcement Agents knew

how to contact them for the questions they'd inevitably need to ask to complete their investigation. Then he and Alyssa headed home. It was a short drive, and Chris knew he wouldn't have much time. He also knew that once he dropped Alyssa off at home, he'd need either a good excuse or an invitation if he wanted to see her again.

He hoped he could get both.

"I know you're going to want to spend a lot of time with you sister," he began.

"I can't wait," Alyssa confirmed. "We have so much catching up to do."

"And I'm sure you're going to be busy with your statues and your art. But I was hoping maybe, even with all of that, maybe I can see you again. Take you out to dinner, or—"

"Like on a date?" Alyssa sounded surprised, but not offended.

"On a date," Chris said with certainty, "a romantic date, with no wailing babies or drug smugglers. Just you and me, maybe some candlelight and good food."

"That sounds completely amazing."

Chris risked a glance her way and then looked back at the road. He'd seen enough of her smile to know she meant the words sincerely. "You're completely amazing." He met her gaze just long enough to see in her eyes the same affection he felt, and his hope soared. If Alyssa's feelings for him were anything like his growing love and admiration of her, he knew the best was yet to come.

EPILOGUE

The cabin echoed with laughter and the warmth of the fire as the snow fell gently outside. Chris and Eric helped Abby and Emma build a long lineup of dominoes to knock down, causing them to squeal with delight every time the game pieces fell with a clatter. Alyssa helped her sister finish washing the last of the dishes from their Christmas Eve dinner, then turned her attention to the eager children who wanted to unwrap the gifts under the tree.

"You can each pick one gift to unwrap tonight," Vanessa explained. "We'll open the rest tomorrow."

Abby and Emma unwrapped the dolls they'd been asking for, and Vanessa was trying to decide which shiny package to unwrap, when the sound of pounding at the door drowned out the laughter and background Christmas music.

"Who would be coming out here on Christmas Eve?" Chris asked.

"Debbi was going caroling with our parents tonight." Eric's brow furrowed. "I don't know who else it could be." Nonetheless, as the technical owner of the cabin, Eric leaped up and answered the door.

"Merry Christmas!" A snow-dusted man stepped in, stomping his boots on the rug.

"Mitch?" Alyssa hadn't seen the DEA agent in weeks,

not since the last time he'd met with her to ask some final questions about the statues that had gone missing. After capturing the drug smugglers, Mitch had come back and taken footprint casts near the ravine where the smugglers had tossed her lamb form, and confiscated the broken form as evidence. But she certainly hadn't expected to see him on Christmas Eve.

"Sorry to interrupt your holiday," Mitch apologized, "but I have something here I thought might make your Christmas even brighter. As you may or may not know, there was a hundred-thousand-dollar reward for information leading to the arrest of the drug smugglers. Because of the testimony you were able to provide for us and the evidence you supplied us with, it's been decided that we couldn't have solved the case without either of you—Vanessa and Alyssa." He pulled out an envelope.

Alyssa watched him in disbelief. Vanessa had been told she'd probably be awarded a large damage settlement from her kidnappers, but due to the lengthy legal process involved, she couldn't expect to see any money for many months, possibly years. In the meantime, she and the girls were staying with Alyssa in the tiny cottage while they got their lives sorted out, and money had been tight.

Mitch lifted the flap on the envelope, and Alyssa saw a check with more zeroes than she'd ever seen on such a document before. "We get to split the reward?" she guessed.

"No," Mitch corrected, struggling to pull the check from the envelope. He tugged the glove from his right hand, then removed the check. As he held it out toward them, his fingers fanned the papers. There were two checks. "You each get the full reward."

Alyssa could only stare, unbelieving, as Vanessa accepted the checks and carried one over to her sister. "Seriously?" Alyssa looked at the document, then to Mitch. "Don't you deserve some of this?"

"I'm an employee." He held up his hands in an innocent gesture. "It's my job."

"Well, thank you!" Vanessa found her voice first. "I didn't expect anything."

"Merry Christmas," Mitch told them again. "I need to get going."

Everyone thanked him heartily again, and he went on his way. For a few moments they simply stared at their checks in wonderment, while the little girls giggled gleefully. Then Eric pulled a large gift-wrapped box out from under the tree, holding it out to Vanessa. "This may seem slightly anticlimactic now, but I'd like you to open this one first."

Vanessa carefully removed the shiny paper to reveal a beautiful nativity set, complete with shepherds and wise men.

"Open it up. Take a look," Eric encouraged her as she thanked him for the lovely gift.

Removing the Styrofoam packing forms, Vanessa opened each in turn, delighting over the lovely figurines. When she opened the section that contained the wise men, she paused. "That's not frankincense." She set the lid to the side and held out the wise man so everyone could see what he held in his hand. Unlike the two other wise men, who held small chests, this one held a round container. Encircling the decorative jar was something Alyssa guessed hadn't come with the set.

A diamond ring.

Eric beamed at Vanessa. She looked up at him and blinked back tears. He lifted the ring from the wise man's offering and held it out toward Vanessa's left hand.

"Will you marry me?" he asked.

For a moment, Vanessa simply stared at his face in wonder.

"Oh, Mommy!" Emma spoke up. "Say yes!"

"Yes, Mommy! Say yes!" Abby chimed in.

Vanessa laughed—the kind of laughter that sounded like happiness bubbling over. "Yes, yes!"

Eric slid the ring on her finger and kissed her, then pulled her into his arms and whispered, "Merry Christmas."

Alyssa wiped happy tears from her eyes as she watched the pair. Finally, she glanced at Chris and saw him crouching by the tree, bouncing on his heels, his hand pressed to his mouth in an indecisive pose. "What?" she asked him quietly.

"I don't know." He laughed an uncertain laugh and shook his head. "I don't know. I was going to wait until Christmas morning, but now feels like the right time." He stood, picked his way across the gifts and wrapping paper that cluttered the floor, and pulled Alyssa's Christmas stocking from the mantel.

For the first time, Alyssa realized there was a squareish bulge in the toe. Her eyes went wide as she watched Chris cross the room toward her. They'd been seeing quite a lot of each other since the smugglers had been caught. Their first date had led to many more, and she couldn't imagine life without him.

But she hadn't been expecting the small, square box that she pulled from the toe of her Christmas stocking as he held it out to her, watching her face expectantly as she freed it from its hiding place and opened the lid.

A diamond ring twinkled inside.

"I thought about trying to hide it in one of your statues," Chris confessed, "but then you'd have to break it to get it out." He looked over at Vanessa and Eric. "The nativity scene was brilliant. I wish I'd thought of that." He met her eyes. "It's not anything too special. Just a ring and my promise to love you forever. Will you marry me?"

Alyssa's hands trembled as she stared at him past the ring, hardly believing that this great guy—whose amazing dimples kept winking at her—wanted her to be his wife.

"Say yes!" Abby and Emma cheered, doubly excited now. Even little Sammy, who was too young to know what was going on, babbled encouragingly.

"Yes," Alyssa whispered, then found her voice and spoke again. "Yes!"

Chris slipped the ring onto her finger and pulled her into his arms. "Merry Christmas," he told her and kissed her, causing her nieces to squeal happily.

Then Alyssa looked down at the ring and into the face of the man she loved and at the family she never thought she'd have. The room was just as cluttered as her statue room. The people in it even looked like her statues. But these were living, breathing people who made her life infinitely richer, not just with their presence, but with their love.

She looked over at the sister she thought she'd never see again and thanked God for bringing her home again. Then she looked into the face of the man she loved and leaned forward as he leaned toward her. He kissed her softly, slowly, then whispered, "I love you."

"I love you," she whispered back, as though the words were too precious to speak aloud.

"Merry Christmas!" Abby squealed, her happiness bubbling over.

"Merry Christmas," Emma chimed in.

Alyssa held Chris's hand and met his eyes again. "Merry Christmas."

* * * * *

Dear Reader,

Eight years is a long time to hold on to hope, especially without any encouraging signs or tangible reasons to believe a situation will change. Even Vanessa and Alyssa confessed that, during their long separation, they'd given up hope of ever seeing each other again.

Have you been holding on to hope for a long time? Does it sometimes feel as though it's been too long—that surely God would have acted by now, if indeed God was willing and able to act?

I have experienced that same doubt in my life, wondering why God hasn't come through, or if things are ever going to turn out according to my hopes and dreams. It can be overwhelming, even faith-crushing, to endure such long waits.

But, as Vanessa and Alyssa's story reminds us, all those long days, months, even years of waiting don't necessarily mean God isn't going to act on our behalf. And the length of time we have to wait can make us that much more grateful in the end—if we haven't allowed ourselves to become embittered by waiting. My prayer for all of us today is that our trust would be as big as the God in whom we trust, and our patience sufficient to see us through to the happy ending in store for us.

Blessings,

Rachelle

Questions for Discussion

1. Vanessa Jackson has been held against her will for eight years. What do you think about her decision to escape as men arrive to murder the man who's held her captive?

2. Knowing Virgil and his associates will probably try to come after them, Vanessa leaves her son, Sammy, with her sister. Does her plan make sense to you? What might you have done differently under the circumstances?

3. When Alyssa first discovers the baby in her manger and reads the message on his shirt, she admits to Chris that she'd never seen the child before. What would you have done in her situation?

4. The baby in the manger renews Alyssa's hope. What kind of symbolism can you find in these elements of the story?

5. Which couple do you like better—Eric and Vanessa, or Chris and Alyssa? Do you think both couples will live happily ever after?